Rescued For Love

Donna Deloney

Proverbial Press
CHICAGO, ILLINOIS

Copyright © 2018 by Donna Deloney.

All rights reserved. No part of this publication may be reproduced, distributed or transmitted in any form or by any means, including photocopying, recording, or other electronic or mechanical methods, without the prior written permission of the publisher, except in the case of brief quotations embodied in critical reviews and certain other noncommercial uses permitted by copyright law. For permission requests, write to the publisher, addressed "Attention: Permissions Coordinator," at the address below.

Proverbial Press
12418 S. Harvard
Chicago, IL 60628

Publisher's Note: This is a work of fiction. Names, characters, places, and incidents are a product of the author's imagination. Locales and public names are sometimes used for atmospheric purposes. Any resemblance to actual people, living or dead, or to businesses, companies, events, institutions, or locales is completely coincidental.

Book Layout ©2013 BookDesignTemplates.com

Ordering Information:
Quantity sales. Special discounts are available on quantity purchases by corporations, associations, and others. For details, contact the "Special Sales Department" at the address above.

Rescued for Love / Donna Deloney. -- 1st ed.
ISBN 978-1-7967854-6-3

*Dedicated to the family and friends
of all Law Enforcement Officials
who have lost their lives in the line of duty.
May they rest in peace.
Thank you for your service.
May God keep all who serve safe from harm.*

*"For I know the plans I have for you," says the Lord.
"They are plans for good and not for disaster,
to give you a future and a hope."*

—JEREMIAH 29:11 (NLT)

CHAPTER ONE

Wake up!

Brianna jolted awake, her heart pounding. Had the bus arrived at school already? She looked around, confused. They were still on the highway. Most of the kids had either fallen asleep or were plugged into their electronics. The other adult chaperon was asleep. The driver was fully awake, humming to himself, eyes fixed on the road ahead. She must have imagined it. Just like sometimes she swore she could hear her mother calling her name, even though she was living peacefully with her father in Atlanta, twelve hours away from Chicago.

Annoyed, Brianna sighed and popped in her earphones. They had another thirty minutes before they'd exit the expressway to school. A catnap would be just what she needed to deal with her rambunctious students when they returned, well rested from the hours-long return trip from a visit to a local college.

She closed her eyes and leaned back, trying to get back into her once comfortable spot on her seat.

BRIANNA, WAKE UP!!

Her eyes popped open. This time, she heard and felt the voice. It was the Holy Spirit trying to get her attention. She sat up, fully awake. Okay, Lord, you have my attention. What's up?

LOOK AHEAD. PAY ATTENTION. BE READY.

She wrapped her headphones around her phone. Slipping out of her seat, she made her way to the front of the bus, gripping the seat backs as she went. She got to the front of the bus and crouched in the seat beside her colleague, Elizabeth Trujillo, who stirred. "Are we there yet?" she mumbled.

"Not yet, Liz," Brianna replied. She stared into the distant traffic, but nothing seemed amiss. She tapped the driver on the shoulder. "Everything okay up here, Ron?"

The man nodded. "Yeah, everything's fine, Ms. Norwood, except for a few idiots who don't know how to drive. But everything's cool."

Ron had been driving for the school for twenty years. He was the consummate professional and Brianna had every confidence in him. But she knew what she had heard. She turned back and forth in her seat, trying to see something. Everything was most definitely not cool.

Liz felt Brianna's restlessness, so she sat up. "What's wrong, Bri?"

"I don't know," Brianna replied. "I just have a feeling…" Her stomach flipped flopped as she pointed out the front window. "There!"

3 | DONNA DELONEY

Liz peered around the driver to see what her friend was pointing at. Her olive skin paled when she saw the car hurtling toward them the wrong way and flying like a missile.

"Everyone," Brianna yelled, "brace for impact!"

CHAPTER TWO

State trooper Jake Lewis pushed his foot on the gas pedal as far as it could go. The call that had come on the radio had rattled him to the core. A driver—drunk, high, unbalanced, or worse, intentional—was flying down the highway at an insane rate of speed, zigzagging through traffic, forcing drivers off the road. The lucky ones were the ones he didn't hit. Last word was that he had crossed the grassy median and was heading thru wrong-way traffic. This was not going to end well. He prayed that somehow the driver would be the only casualty.

The traffic was slowing, so he knew there must have been some sort of an accident. As the cars in the two left lanes began merging to the right, he sped along the middle shoulder. Up ahead a few hundred feet, he could see smoke billowing. Grabbing his mic, he identified himself then called out, "Heading northbound on 94, mile marker 181. I'm seeing smoke up ahead in the southbound lanes. Roll fire and EMS."

"Copy," the dispatcher responded. "Rolling fire and EMS. Can you confirm casualties?"

"Negative. Should have a better estimate in two." He kept his eyes focused on the road ahead, trying to zero in on where the smoke was coming from. In the opposite lanes, he could see cars trying to get back on the road, having escaped the offending driver. He crossed the median at the first open entrance and gasped. His worse fears had been realized. The mangled car was grotesquely intertwined with the front end of a school bus, which was lying on its side. Jake could see smoke rising from the two engine blocks and the slow burn of an orange flame was peeking from the hood of the car. He hopped out of his car, grabbed the fire extinguisher, ran over to the vehicles and doused out the flame. He knocked out the glass of the driver's window of the car and checked on the driver. Dead. He said a quick prayer for the man's soul, but stopped as he heard cries coming from the bus. Another flame appeared, this one a lot larger and spreading quickly through the debris. He debated for a moment: should he try and extinguish the flames, or tend to the victims on the bus? Either way, he was sure he didn't have time to do both. He perked up as he heard sirens in the distance and could see a fire crew in route. Problem solved. He was needed at the bus.

He dropped the extinguisher and ran to the emergency exit at the rear of the bus. He tugged on the handle—jammed! He could hear the cries and moans of the passengers inside. "God help," he pleaded.

CHAPTER THREE

Brianna forced her eyes open, ignoring the pounding in her head. She felt something wet on her face and touched it. Blood. Not surprising considering... *Oh God! We were in an accident!* She tried to focus, but it was difficult to clear her thoughts with the blinding pain in her head. It was the screams of her students that finally snapped her into complete consciousness. She realized the bus was lying on its side. She could see smoke rising from the engine block. Her eyes widened when she saw flames licking the crumpled remains of the vehicle that had plowed into them.

"Liz, we have to get the kids out," Brianna said. In the dark, she could barely see. Feeling around, she saw her friend lying in a bizarre angle, unmoving. She felt for a pulse and thanked God there was one. It was weak, but it meant Liz was still alive. But there wasn't much time. Brianna was sure of that.

"Who's near the exit? Who's in the back?" The kids were in various states of shock and panic. She had to get them under control or they'd never get out in time. "Hey! Listen up, right now!"

"Ms. Norwood! We have to get outta here! We're gonna die," one of the girls called out.

"No, we're not! We're getting out of here. I need everyone to listen to me and do exactly as I say!" She paused a second but could hear the kids settling down. Her months of working with them were finally paying off and she had their attention. "Who's in the back by the exit? Call out!"

"It's me, Ms. Norwood, me and Logan," a young man's voice called out.

Bryce and Logan. Football players. Muscular build. "Bryce, are you hurt?"

"I'm good," Bryce responded.

"Me too," Logan called out.

"Great! If you can move, get that rear exit open as quickly as possible! We've got to get everyone off the bus." As best as she could see, the two boys were maneuvering in place to get the door opened. "The rest of you, if you can move, try and make your way to the rear of the bus. If someone next to you is hurting, try to assist them." She coughed. *The bus is filling with smoke. Help us, Lord.* "How are you coming with that door, boys?"

"It's jammed," Bryce called out. He coughed. "What do we do?"

"Break the window!"

"With what?"

"I don't know," Brianna replied. "Kick it out if you have to, but we've got to get a way out now!"

Logan yelled, "Give me your jacket, B." His teammate quickly pulled off his windbreaker and handed it over to Logan, who wrapped it around his arm, which was already wrapped in his own jacket. "Look out!" With his powerful forearm, he smashed the glass, which shattered. He cleared the glass from the frame, then called out, "Marcus, come here!"

A tall, lean, dark-skinned boy found his way to the back. "What's up?"

"You think you can make it through?"

"Heck yeah, I'll get through," Marcus replied.

"Okay, you get out and when we count three, you pull and we're gonna blaze through."

"Gotcha, dawg." Marcus shimmied through the window, collapsing on the ground below. He quickly got up and grabbed on the door handle and waited.

"On three, B. One, two, three!" Logan and Bryce powered into the door like they were taking down an opposing defense on the football field. With Marcus yanking on the other side, the door flew open, with the three young men tumbling to the ground.

"Okay," Brianna yelled, "everyone that can move, go now! Move towards the rear exit! Help each other out the door!" The remaining children needed no further prompting. She saw them making their way towards the emergency exit, some walking, some crawling, others helping the more severely injured or dazed to the rear.

The smoke was growing thicker by the second. Brianna had the urge to head out herself, but she remembered her friends, Liz and Ron. They hadn't stirred at all. She got to Liz first, who was moaning, but still not fully conscious. Brianna gripped her under the arms and began dragging the woman towards the rear. She stumbled over the backpacks that were strewn about the overturned bus. The fumes from the smoke began to overpower and she fought to stay upright. She collapsed to her knees, her coughing turning into spasms. Her eyes were burning, but she kept tugging, trying to drag Liz to the open. She nearly toppled over, but then felt a strong arm lifting her up. "I got you, Ms. Norwood," Bryce called out. "Get outta here."

"Liz," was all she managed to get out.

"We got her," Logan replied. He moved around her and positioned himself at Liz's head, as Bryce maneuvered towards her legs. "Go, Ms. Norwood, go!"

Brianna nodded and began crawling towards the exit. As she moved, she felt along, trying to determine if any students were still on the bus. As best she could tell, everyone made it out.

"Go Ms. Norwood," Bryce called out, "or we'll never make it! Everyone got out!"

Brianna tried to acknowledge them, but instead of words, all she could do was cough savagely. She picked up the pace, noting that the boys were starting to feel the effects of the smoke. As she made her way to the exit, she could hear a popping noise that sounded like sparks from behind her. *The engine's going to catch fire! The bus is going to explode!* She tumbled out of the bus and into the arms of a man in a uniform. She righted herself and began pointing at the bus. The man started dragging her away, but Brianna used what little of her strength left to pull away from him. She staggered towards the bus, just as Bryce and Logan climbed out with a still unconscious Liz. She tapped Logan's shoulder. "Ev—ev'ry—body out?"

Logan nodded. "We all got out." He paused, coughing and trying to get his breath.

"We did a head count," Bryce added. "It was just you and Ms. Trujillo and–"

"Ron!" Brianna cried out. "He's still inside!" She lunged for the bus, but was restrained by the man in uniform.

"You can't go in there," he said. "There's no time!"

"Let me go! I have to go get Ron!" Brianna tried to pull away but the last of her strength was gone. He forcibly dragged her away from the wreckage.

"Miss, I can't let you go back in there! Fellas, move the lady back this way," he directed the boys. "Everybody get back! Move back!"

At that moment, the front of the bus erupted into flames. There was a loud explosion that nearly knocked everyone down. The man kept tugging at Brianna, who kept resisting. "Ma'am, I'm sorry. It's too late."

"Ron! RON!!! Noooo…." Brianna moaned. A wave a dizziness overtook her, but she managed to pull away from the uniformed officer. "You! You should have let me get him! Or you should have tried to save him! This is your fault! This is…" Another wave of dizziness hit. Before she could stop herself, Brianna collapsed in the stranger's arms.

CHAPTER FOUR

A spasm of coughing roused Brianna into consciousness. Her first semi-conscious thought was pain. Everything hurt, especially her head. She could barely open her eyes, as the light seemed to increase the throbbing she felt. Another cough sent another ripple of pain through her body. *What happened? Where am I?* She was acutely aware that her breathing was somewhat labored and there was some sort of mask on her face. She forced her eyes open and glanced around the room, trying her best not to move her head. She saw an IV tube running in one arm and monitors positioned to the left of the bed. A woman in scrubs leaned over and smiled. "Welcome back. You're going to be just fine."

"Where…"

The woman rested her hand on Brianna's shoulder. "You're at Christ Medical Center. You were in a bus accident and they transported you here. You had a pretty nasty gash on your head and a concussion. You also inhaled quite a bit of smoke. But you're going to be okay."

Bus accident! Flashes of the day's events filtered through her mind. "The kids… they're safe?"

The woman nodded. "As far as I know. A lot of cuts and bruises, some broken bones. One child had a pretty serious skull fracture, but last I heard, everyone made it."

"Liz? Ron?"

"Who?"

"Liz—Elizabeth Trujillo. She's the other teacher on the bus. And Ronald Brewer. He's the driver."

The nurse frowned. "I'll have to check on them. I'll find out. In the meantime, you just rest. The doctor will be in shortly to talk with you." She handed her a small remote. "If you want to watch some TV, here you go. The button on the right side of the bed will connect you to the nurse's station." She smiled again, checked the monitors and exited the room.

Brianna sighed. There was nothing for her to do except lay in the bed. She glanced at the clock on the wall. It was nearly 6:00 p.m.! Her students' parents must have been worried sick! But, she realized, the school must have been notified about the accident, which meant parents were probably already at the hospital. But what about Liz's husband? And Ron's wife? Had they been called too?

Brianna chuckled at the irony of her thoughts. Who had been notified on her behalf? No one close by. Her parents were traveling overseas yet again. Other than a couple of her cousins in Milwaukee, there was nobody close enough to care. Her ex-boyfriend, Pete? Ha. It wouldn't even register with him. No, other than her best friend, Liz, there was no one around that would be there for her. At the moment, she couldn't decide if she was happy or sad about the thought.

Enough of this. I'm alive. My kids are alive. It could have been so much worse. Thank you, Lord, for your protection. She turned on the TV just in time for the evening newscast.

"Tonight's top stories," the anchor began, "begins with a horrific crash on the Bishop Ford involving an out of control vehicle and a school bus." Brianna turned the volume up. According to the anchor, the vehicle had been weaving in and out of traffic at a high rate of speed before crossing the median and slamming into the bus. "Police have not identified the driver of the vehicle, nor have they determined if the driver was driving erratically due to a mechanical failure, intoxication, or as an act of terror. State police have stated the driver of the vehicle was pronounced dead at the scene. Miraculously, everyone on the bus was able to exit the vehicle before it exploded, suffering mostly non-life-threatening injuries." The anchor moved on to the next story with hardly a breath in between.

Brianna slammed her hand in frustration. What about Ron? The anchor didn't mention if he made it out or not. She willed the nurse to return with some news on Liz and Ron. At that moment, the doctor walked in to check on her. "Hi, I'm Dr. Benton. How are you doing?"

"You tell me, Doc," Brianna answered, with what she hoped was a smile. She coughed some, but it didn't hurt as bad

"Well, based on what I can see, you're going to be fine. We want to keep you overnight for observation because of the concussion and smoke inhalation. But unless there are complications, we should have you out of here sometime tomorrow."

"Can I take off this mask?"

He nodded. "I think so. Your PO2 levels have stabilized for the most part, but I want you to stay on oxygen through the night, just to be safe. I'll have the nurse come back in and switch you to a nasal cannula. That should be sufficient. However, if you have more coughing or breathing issues, we'll have to put the mask back on you. If you're hungry, let the nurse know and she can have something brought up to you. Any questions for me?"

Brianna shook her head. "I'm just waiting to hear about my friends from the bus."

"I'll have the nurse check for you. I'll see you tomorrow." As Dr. Benton turned to exit, the door to her room swung open. Liz entered, sitting in a wheelchair guided by her husband, Luis. "Gracias, el Dio!" Liz exclaimed. Luis parked Liz's chair next to Brianna's bed, and she grasped her friend's hand. "Oh, thank the Lord you're okay! I've been so worried about you!"

"Same here," Brianna whispered, tears rolling down her face. "They wouldn't tell me what happened to you. Are you okay?"

Liz shrugged. "As well as can be expected. A lot of bumps and bruises, but nothing serious. Well, except for one heck of a headache. What about you?"

"Same. I ache all over, like I did one of those obstacle courses we see on TV all the time." The nurse came in and quickly switched Brianna's oxygen mask for the cannula. Once she made sure Brianna was okay, she showed her the menu and told her to order when she was ready. "Have you seen any of the kids? Talked to any parents," Brianna asked.

Liz shook her head. "They're scattered all over the hospital, at least the ones who haven't been released already. I asked the nurse to help me track them down and she said she would let me know."

"I owe you a debt of thanks," Luis said. His dark eyes filled with tears. "If you hadn't pulled Liz out of the bus, I don't know what I would have done." He leaned over and kissed his wife on top of her head.

"I'd like to take credit, but it was actually Bryce and Logan who did the work," Brianna replied.

"Yes, but they told me you stayed behind to get her out and you were dragging her out."

"I tried my best. But if they hadn't come when they did, I don't know if either of us would have made it out."

"Well, if they think saving my life will get them an A in my class," Liz said, chuckling, "they are sorely mistaken. They *might* get a B out of me." That made everyone laugh, but Brianna started coughing at the end.

"You okay, Bri?"

"Yeah, just need some water. My throat is dry."

Luis saw a pitcher with water on a table and poured her a cup. He handed it to Brianna, who took a sip. "Delicious."

There was a knock at the door. "Come on in, the party's in here," Brianna called out. The first thing Brianna noticed was his smooth, dark brown skin. He had beautiful dimples that showed, even though his smile was small. His eyes—dark brown, but full of compassion—made Brianna catch her breath. Even as she took in the sight of his state trooper uniform, she could see he was well built. "May I help you?"

"Mrs. Norwood?"

"Yes, but it's Miss." Brianna ignored Liz's snickering. "What can I do for you, Officer?"

"I'm Trooper Jake Lewis with the Illinois State Police. I was first on the scene of the accident."

Brianna frowned. Something in his voice was familiar. She stared at him, trying to put it together. "You were there?"

"Yes, ma'am. I assisted you after you made out of the bus."

Suddenly, it clicked. "You. You grabbed me. You wouldn't let me go back in after Ron."

Jake nodded. "I couldn't let you take that chance. The fire department had just arrived on scene. I thought it best to let them do their job. And you were in no condition to do much of anything, much less rescue anyone trapped inside."

"Did he get out?"

"Who?"

"Ronnie Brewster, the driver. Did they get him out?"

Jake shook his head. "They did, but I'm sorry; he didn't make it."

Brianna covered her eyes as the tears fell. "You should have let me go back in there."

"I couldn't."

"Then you should have gone in for him!"

"It wouldn't have made any difference. My going in after him would have hindered the fire department's operations. It was my job to make sure that you and your students got to safety. And I'm sorry that I couldn't save your friend. But I won't apologize for doing my job."

"Could you just go? Please?" Brianna leaned back in her bed. The tears were flowing in earnest. "I can't deal with you right now."

"Miss Norwood…"

"Please, just go!"

Luis went over to Jake. "Maybe it's best you leave right now." He began walking the trooper to the door.

"I'm sorry. I didn't mean to upset her."

"It's just been a really emotional day. She'll be alright once she has time to process everything that's happened."

"I hate to leave her like this."

"It's okay. Liz and I will be here for her. Thank you for coming by and giving us the news. And thank you for what you did to save their lives. I am eternally grateful. And Brianna will be too, once she's come to terms with this. You have to understand. Everyone at that school is like family."

"What school?"

"Trinity Christian High. Ron wasn't just a bus driver. He was a tutor, coach, mentor, and a good friend. He and his wife took Brianna under their wing when she first came to the school. In many ways, he was like a father to her."

"I see," Jake said, sympathy filling his eyes. "Then losing him was a considerable blow."

"Si," Luis replied. "But Trinity will come together in prayer and seek God's peace and comfort."

"Add my prayers to yours."

"You're a believer?"

"I am," Jake said, warmly.

Luis grasped his hand. "Then you're our brother. And we will lift you up in prayer as well. Do you mind if I pray for you?"

"Only if you'll let me do the same for you," Jake said, bowing his head.

"Amen," Luis replied.

One year later…

CHAPTER FIVE

"Oh, my goodness, she is so beautiful," Brianna declared. She held Liz's two-month old daughter close to her chest. "I love how babies smell. And look at all this hair!" She cooed at the sleeping baby. "I'm glad I get to be her godmother."

"We're glad you accepted," Liz said, smiling. "We couldn't think of a better person to share in raising Isabella in the faith. And of course, it helps that I'm an only child," she added.

"There's that. And Luis' brother is her godfather?"

Liz frowned. "Ugh, yes. His mother insisted. I like Ronaldo well enough, but his faith is shaky at best, and his walk is non-existent, as far as I'm concerned." She sighed. "But he adores Bella. And he's loaded. So, there's that. And, God forbid, if anything happens to us, Ronaldo will make sure she has everything she needs. But you will be her legal guardian. Luis and I made that clear to both our families. It's in our wills."

Brianna stared down at her goddaughter. *Please, dear God, for Bella's sake, let her parents stick around for a long, long time.*

"You're not having second thoughts, are you?" Luis asked, as he entered the living room with two cups of coffee.

"Nope. Just praying for your health and long life," Brianna replied.

Luis handed his wife her mug, kissed her, then set Brianna's mug in front of her. "You want me to take her?"

"No, not yet. These are best moments."

"Yes, they are. Stick around for the fun stuff when she's stinking up her diapers and puking on my shirt."

Brianna chuckled. "Don't you listen to him, Bella. He loves every minute of it."

"I love her; she can keep the puke. I'm gonna go watch some TV while you ladies chat." He leaned over and kissed his daughter. "Call me if you need anything."

Liz took a sip of her coffee. "Mmmm…" She rolled her eyes in bliss. "I have missed this."

"Coffee?"

"Yes. And talk about anything other than the baby." She saw the confusion on her friend's face. "Don't get me wrong. I love my baby girl. Having her has brought me so much joy and happiness. But I was no hurry to have kids, y'know? After the accident, Luis and I realized we shouldn't put off waiting for tomorrow. But I miss teaching, interacting with kids who can answer back."

"Even if they're being disrespectful?"

"That's the beauty of it. They are teaching me how to handle Bella when she gets older. But it's not just that. I want to get out of the house. I need to stimulate my mind on grown up things. Plus, I miss us hanging out. I miss my life."

Brianna smiled. "What a life. I'd trade places with you in a heartbeat."

"You say that now, but wait until you are completely ignored and the only conversation you have with other adults is how well the baby pooped."

Brianna laughed, causing Bella to stir. "You're really coming back to work next week?"

"Sure am. I know Bella will be in great hands. My mom will be here for three days a week and Luis' mom will be with her the other two days. They absolutely love spoiling their only granddaughter, and I love knowing she's not with strangers. Plus, they are both wonderful cooks!"

"That's terrific, Liz. And I'm personally glad you're coming back. I've missed hanging out with you too. Your sub is such a Debbie Downer. The kids hate her."

"Perfect! Then they'll appreciate me more now that I'm coming back. Now, catch me up on everything. What's happening at school?"

"The career fair is next week. I volunteered to help Ms. Richardson put it together. We've got all kinds of terrific speakers lined up. Some professionals, a couple of CEOs, some small business entrepreneurs, and of course, your requisite doctors, lawyers, police officers. I just hope none of the kids really get involved with the police."

"Why not? It's an honorable profession, even if there are few rotten apples."

"It used to be. Look at all the police shootings and murders of innocent people. All the videos of police brutality! And what about the dangers they face every day? Those cops in Dallas and New

Orleans and New York who were killed simply because they wore a badge? No, I would never steer any of my kids to become a cop."

"Everything you said is true, Bri," Liz countered. "But the majority of police officers are doing their jobs and doing them well. And they are under a lot of pressure. They need our support. I know there needs to be changes in the police departments around the country. It starts from within. And maybe, just maybe, we need more police who know Christ and who see police work as a call to service. If we have more of them on the force, maybe their lights will shine and drive the darkness away from the police, *sí?*"

"*Sí*," Brianna responded. "You're right, I suppose. I won't discourage anyone who wants to become a cop. But I'm sure not encouraging anyone either."

CHAPTER SIX

From the moment Brianna arrived at Trinity on Monday morning, she was firing on all cylinders. In addition to prepping for her English classes, she was helping Lisa Richardson, the school's college and career counselor, to coordinate the career fair, which was scheduled to take place during fourth through seventh periods, when study halls and lunch occurred. Brianna had already confirmed her guests for the day. The only one she didn't have a specific name for was the representative from the Illinois State Police. Their director for media affairs had been on vacation, and his deputy had only confirmed that someone from the force would be in attendance and ready to speak.

She checked the cafeteria and found Ms. Richardson had all the tables lined up and tagged with each organization or company being represented. She was proud of the fact that many of the speakers were of color, which she hoped would help her students connect with the potential career opportunities. Being African

American herself, Brianna knew the importance of seeing people who looked like her seated in a position of authority. No one had cheered more loudly on that November evening in 2008 when Barack and Michelle Obama took the stage with their daughters at the victory celebration in Grant Park. There was tremendous jubilation among most of the staff and students the next day. Oh sure, some grumbled because their guy had lost, but most were in awe that an African American had been elected president of the United States. Brianna always used the Obamas as examples for students that there was nothing they couldn't achieve if they worked hard enough.

Today, though, Brianna just wanted to make sure everything went smoothly. She was thrilled to have Liz back and they promised to check in with each other during lunch. As she prepped her classroom, she began humming a praise and worship song she heard from yesterday's morning worship service. By the time the first bell rang and her first period students strolled in, she was in such a wonderful mood, she just knew nothing would bring her down.

By the time she made it to the cafeteria at the start of fourth period, she had to control herself to keep from dancing down the hallway. She greeted each presenter warmly, taking a brief moment to check out their displays and seeing if there was anything they needed. She stopped short as she noticed the representative from the Illinois State Police. Her heart began beating faster and she willed herself to stand perfectly still. *It can't be him. It just can't be him. Of all the officers in the state of Illinois, why did they send him?*

"What's wrong?" Liz asked, sidling up to her friend's side. "I'd say you were pale as a ghost, but black girls don't go pale."

"It's him," Brianna muttered, barely moving her lips.

"Him? Who?"

"Him. From last year."

"What him? Where?"

"Over there, at the state police booth," Brianna said, imperceptibly nodding her head in the man's direction.

Liz scanned the booth, then broke into a smile. "Oh, you mean Jake?"

Brianna whirled around. "You remember him?"

"Yeah, he stopped by your hospital room."

"Yeah, but you act like you know him know him."

"I do. He and Luis became prayer partners. He's been to the house a couple of times."

"You're friends? And you've had him to your house? How come you never told me?"

Liz shrugged. "I didn't think it was a big deal. He'd come over sometimes and watch football with Luis and the guys."

"He wasn't at your Super Bowl party."

"He had to work that day. And why are you freaking out? He's a good guy. And he helped to save our lives."

"And Ron lost his," Brianna countered, holding back tears.

Liz placed a hand on her friend's shoulder. "You know that was not his fault. Ron died on impact, and you know that. The autopsy proved that. And if Jake had gone in or let you go back in, you'd both be just as dead as Ron, and that would be his fault."

"Still..."

"Let it go, Bri. Ask God to give you peace about this. He had a tough decision to make and it wasn't easy for him. You don't think he carries some guilt about that day? The truth is, he wishes he could have saved Ron. But he couldn't, just like you couldn't."

"I know. In my head, I know. But in my heart… when I see him, it just reminds of me of that day and who we lost."

"Then it's up to you to change it. Let seeing him remind you of the life you have now. I know I'm grateful." She smiled. "It's time to suck it up, buttercup. You're a professional. Pull up your big girl panties, slap a smile on your face and greet your guest. And remember, he's one of the good guys!"

Brianna nodded. Liz was right. If nothing else, she had to treat him as professionally as she would any of the other presenters. She faked as big of a grin as she could, causing Liz to roll her eyes in dismay. "What's his name, Jack?"

"It's Jake. Jake Lewis. Be nice," Liz warned.

"I'm always nice." She turned back around, squared her shoulders and marched over to where Jake stood chatting with a couple of students. She waited as he spoke earnestly about the job of a police officer, especially one with the state police. From his tone, it was clear that he was passionate about his career. He was also an inspiring speaker. Brianna noticed he had completely captivated the students who were gathered at the table. When he was done, he handed them some informational literature, and a couple of marketing items he'd brought with him. When one of the boys asked for an application, Jake asked, "What year are you?"

"Senior," the young man replied.

"How old are you?"

"Seventeen, but I'll be eighteen next week."

"That's great, man. Happy birthday! Unfortunately, we don't take applicants before the age of twenty-one." Seeing the look of disappointment on the young man's face, he added. "However, we do have an internship program that you can apply for. But you have continued your education. Once you earn your degree, you'll be a great candidate for the academy in a couple of years." He handed the boy his card. "Here's my contact information. Shoot me an email and we'll talk more about your career path and how best to get you there."

"Thank you, Sergeant," the boy said. The two of them shook hands and the boy headed back to his table. He turned his attention to Brianna. His smile grew wider. "Miss Norwood, right?"

Brianna nodded. "That's right. I'm surprised you remember me."

It was impossible to forget you. "You definitely look better than the last time I saw you." *Oh crap. Where did that come from?*

Fortunately, Brianna laughed. "I'd like to think so. You definitely didn't see me on my best day." *Whoa there, girl. Back away.* "I'm not just talking about how I looked. I owe you an apology."

"It's not necessary."

"Yes, it is. Please let me finish." He nodded and she continued. "I shouldn't have blamed you for what happened to Ron. It wasn't your fault and nothing you could have done would have changed the outcome. I was incredibly rude. You didn't deserve that, and I'm sorry. Please forgive me."

"Forgiven and forgotten. How about we start over?" He extended his hand, which she took. "Sergeant Jake Lewis, Illinois State Police. And you are?"

"Brianna Norwood, teacher and assistant coordinator of this shindig. Thank you for coming. And congratulations on the promotion."

"Thank you." Jake knew he should release her hand, but he didn't want the contact to end. Something about her intrigued him. It wasn't just her physical attributes, though they were plenty. Her grip was strong, but her hands were soft. Her blouse and tailored pants accentuated her curves, but were not revealing. Her auburn curls cascaded around her face, and complimented her warm-brown skin. No, it was her eyes: dark, serious, and yet playful. He could sense that about her. Yes, she was a woman of complementary contrasts. He wanted to know more. He *needed* to know more.

"Sergeant?"

He blinked. How long had he been staring? "Yes?"

"I asked if you needed anything? I need to check in with our other presenters."

"Yes. I mean, no."

Brianna smiled. It was the first time she'd seen Jake flustered. "Okay, then. I'll leave you to it." She gave him a puzzled look. "Sergeant?"

"Please, call me Jake."

"Jake?"

"Yes."

"Jake, I need my hand back."

"Oh." He laughed nervously. Brianna found it charming. "I'll see you later," he said, a question in his tone.

She nodded. "Yes, I'll check in with you later." She turned and walked to the next table.

Jake couldn't help himself. Her backside was as beautiful as her front. *Oh yes, I definitely need to know more.* He forced himself to refocus as another student approached his table.

CHAPTER SEVEN

The next morning, and excited Liz caught up to Brianna just as she was getting her morning latte. "Chica, what did you do to Jake?"

"I beg your pardon?"

"I'm asking, what did you do to him?"

"I don't have the foggiest idea what you're talking about, Liz."

"I'm talking about the whammy you put on that poor guy." She laughed at her friend's puzzled expression. "Jake called Luis last night for their weekly prayer call. Luis said all he could talk about was you."

Brianna frowned. "Jake the trooper? Why was he talking about me?"

"Why do you think he was talking about you? You put a whammy, a humina-humina on him, you rocked his world!"

"What is a humina-humina?"

"Girl, quit playing. You know exactly what I'm talking about." Liz leaned back. "Or maybe it's been so long, you've forgotten."

Brianna opened then closed her mouth. Jake was talking about her that way. "Well, we did have a moment yesterday. At least, I thought we had a moment."

"You had more than a moment. I was watching. I could have heated up my lunch with all the electricity you two had."

"Cut it out," Brianna said, laughing.

"I'm serious! When you left, he was watching you. When he didn't have students surrounding him, he was always trying to find you."

"You're serious?"

"Hand to God. That man was feeling you, but good. From what I could see, he would have been more than happy to keep on feeling you." Liz wiggled her eyebrows up and down, causing Brianna to burst out laughing.

"You are too much, Liz. I will admit, he's pretty cute."

"Cute? Baby, you need to have your eyes checked, because brother-man was way more than cute! He's hot!"

"Liz! You're a married woman!"

"Shoot. I'm not knocking Luis, but there's something about a man in a uniform." She mock shuddered. "Anyway, he's more interested in you. The question is, are you interested?"

Brianna shook her head. "I'm not trying to get involved with a police officer. Especially not that one. We have too much history."

Liz rolled her eyes. "Oh please. Are you still on this? Let me ask you this: if he hadn't been involved in the accident, if the first time you met was yesterday at the career fair, would you consider going out with him?"

"Who said anything about going out with him?"

"It's a hypothetical question, which you haven't answered."

"Hypothetically? Maybe. It depends."

"On what?"

"On what exactly he said to Luis."

CHAPTER EIGHT

The rest of Brianna's day went as expected. Her students were eager to share their experiences at the career fair, which she knew was an excuse to avoid talking about the day's lesson. She chuckled when she gave them the assignment to write an essay: "What I Will Be When I Grow Up." Most of the kids groaned at the thought of another writing assignment, especially one they had done in third grade. Brianna felt it was important to capitalize on their enthusiasm and help them crystallize their dreams now that they had more knowledge about their desired professions. She knew that for some, they were already on the road to achieving their goals. Others were still in the exploration stage. She wanted them to know that there were no limitations to their dreams.

She was looking forward to a quiet night of reading and working on her fledgling novel. Hoping to maximize on her free time, she hurried through the halls of the school, dodging lingering students and colleagues wanting to make small talk. As she reached the main office to swipe out for the day, she gave a friendly wave to the school secretary and barreled through the door, only to bump into Jake, who was just coming in. Brianna stooped down to collect her belongings, once again bumping into the trooper, who had knelt down to help.

"I'm sorry about that," Jake said.

"My bad," Brianna answered. "I wasn't watching where I was going." She was annoyed that he had broken up her rhythm. She snatched her cellphone from his hand. Sighing, she said, "I'm sorry. That was rude."

"It's okay," he replied, smiling. As they stood, he could read the irritation on her face. He tried to diffuse the situation with a little humor. "What's that expression about a moving object colliding with an irresistible force?"

He was rewarded with a half-smile. "I suppose you're the irresistible force?"

"I'd like to think so."

She sighed again. "What brings you back, Sergeant? Did you forget something?"

"Ah, no... not exactly." He had to tread carefully not to get back on her bad side. "I, um... I was in the area, and I wanted to see if any other students had expressed interest in learning more about the state police."

Brianna shook her head. "Not that I'm aware of. You can check with the admin at the desk to see if anyone else turned in information forms. Is there anything else, Sergeant?"

"Yes, Miss Norwood." If she was keeping it formal, so would he. "I was wondering if I could buy you a cup of coffee as a way to say thank you for inviting me."

Brianna's jaw dropped. She turned to the admin, who had ducked her head, but couldn't hide the grin on her face. "Let's take this outside, please." She escorted him just outside the main entrance. "Sergeant—"

"Jake, please."

"Jake. I wish you wouldn't have done that."

"Done what?"

"Ask me out." She blushed. "You were asking me out, right?"

"I was trying to."

She paused to collect her thoughts. "I'm flattered, Sergeant."

"Jake."

"I'm flattered, Jake. Really, I am. But I don't think this is a good idea."

"What, coffee?"

"Us." She wiggled a finger between the two of them. "This."

"It's just coffee. Not a lifetime commitment."

"I see."

"And if coffee isn't your thing, we could do something else. Ice cream. Cotton candy. Banana splits. Malteds."

"Malteds? No one serves malteds anymore. That's straight out of a *Happy Days* rerun."

"I love *Happy Days*."

She rolled her eyes, then laughed. "You're a cornball."

"It's one of my many wonderful traits. I'd like to get to know some of yours."

Her smile was genuine. "That was pretty smooth, Jake."

"Is it enough to get you to have coffee with me?"

"Yes, but not today. I have plans."

His smile faltered. "Oh. Okay. I shouldn't have assumed."

"Assumed what? That I'd be free for a last-minute invitation?"

"Well, yes. Luis said you weren't seeing anyone."

"Ah, yes. Luis. Liz said the two of you had been chatting. For the record, I'm not seeing anyone, but I do have plans, and you are holding me up."

"I apologize. I won't hold you up any longer. But before you go," he handed her a card, "my cell number is here. I'd really like to take you out for coffee and conversation, if that works for you. Just let me know when you're free. Have a good evening."

Brianna watched him walk away. "Wait." He turned back and she walked over. "I've got time for a chocolate shake."

CHAPTER NINE

"Hey Des," Jake said, stretching his long legs across his ottoman. "Did I catch you at a bad time?"

Desmond Lewis chuckled. "Nah, I'm good little brother. It's lunch time on the base." Jake's older brother was a sergeant in the Marines and used nearly every break to work out and stay fit to train new recruits.

"Which means I caught you in the middle of a run."

"No running for me today. Twisted my ankle yesterday."

Jake sat up, concerned. "Are you okay?"

"I'm fine. I'm just on desk duty for another few days. About as boring as watching paint dry."

"How did you hurt yourself?"

"I was biking near Kaneohe Bay. Man, it's gorgeous. I can't wait 'til you come to Oahu so I can show you the island. You'll never want to go back to Chicago."

"Des, your ankle?"

"Oh yeah, right. Like I said, I was biking near the bay, when this fine bronze beauty came running right at me. I fell for her–literally."

Jake roared with laughter. "Was she worth it?"

"She's coming over tonight to nurse me back to health."

Jake shook his head. "Same old Des." His brother not changed. Desmond was determined to never settle down. Jake prayed he would find the love of a good woman and mend his wandering ways. It was one area the brothers disagreed on and their faith walks diverged. *Semper fi* was the motto of the Core; it didn't apply to Desmond where women were concerned.

"You know me well. Enough about me. You never call during the middle of the week unless it's my birthday or something's wrong. My birthday isn't for another two months. Did something happen?"

"Something did happen," Jake replied. He couldn't keep the smile out of his voice. "I met her."

"Her? Her who?"

"HER! The woman I told you about last year after the bus accident."

"Oh–you mean the girl who kicked you out of her hospital room without so much as a thank you? That her?"

"Yes–her. Her name is Brianna Norwood. She's a high school writing teacher and she's phenomenal. She's gorgeous. And smart. And talented. And–"

"Yeah, yeah, I get it. She's all that and a bag of chips with a pickle on the side. Just how do you know all of this about her?"

"We went out."

"On a date?"

"Not exactly. I took her out for ice cream."

Now it was Desmond's turn to break out into laughter. "Man, you're still as corny as ever. Haven't I taught you anything?"

"You taught me everything I don't want to do when it comes to women, Des. Besides, I had to think of something to get her to go out with me. She didn't want coffee; ice cream was the compromise. It worked, too. We talked for a couple of hours and she agreed to go out with me again on Saturday."

"Hmmph," Desmond snorted. "I hope you've got something better than ice cream in mind if you want to impress her."

"I know," Jake replied. "I've been doing some research." He quickly laid out his ideas based on what he knew about Brianna and what Luis had told him. "What do you think?"

"Oo-rah!" Desmond yelled. "Go get her, little brother!"

CHAPTER TEN

"So, you went out on your first date. How did it go?" Liz asked, juggling her cell phone on her shoulder as she nursed Bella.

"It was not a date, Liz," Brianna said. She had her phone on speaker as she brushed out her hair. "We just had ice cream."

"It doesn't take two hours to eat an ice cream cone."

"It was a banana split. And how do you know how long it took? Let me guess: Luis."

"Yep. He and Jake talked."

"What did he say?"

"Luis said the man is smitten."

"Smitten?"

"Yes. The question is, are you?"

Brianna shrugged. "I'm intrigued. He's an interesting man. Did you know he volunteers as a tutor at his church? He also coaches little league part-time."

"And he's hot."

"Yes, that too," Brianna said, laughing.

"Does this mean you're going to give him a chance?"

"I'm going out with him on Saturday."

"Woo hoo! I knew you two would hit it off."

***

It was unusually warm for April. Brianna couldn't decide how she should dress. Jake said to dress casually, but he wouldn't tell her where they were going. She hadn't been this nervous in years. It occurred to her that she really cared how she looked for Jake. She finally settled on a short-sleeve blouse with a multicolor print, a pair of jeans and a black blazer. She didn't think gym shoes would work with the outfit, so she added a pair of black ballet flats. With the right coordinated jewelry, she was set for almost anything Jake decided on.

After their ice cream outing, Jake insisted she call him when she got home so he knew she was in safely. She couldn't decide if it was due to the hazards of his profession or if he was truly being chivalrous. Maybe it was a combination of both. In any case, Brianna liked it.

Today, he insisted on picking her up, so she reluctantly gave him her address. He promised he'd be at her house at by 11:30. At 11:15, the doorbell rang. *He's early. Good thing I'm ready.* She felt her heart race at the thought of seeing Jake again. *Slow down, easy girl. It's just one date.* Smiling, she opened the door. "You're—" Her jaw dropped. "What are you doing here?"

Standing in front of her, wearing a sheepish grin, stood her ex-boyfriend, Peter Bradford. "Hey baby! Wooo, you're looking hot!"

"Again, what are you doing here, Pete?"

45 | DONNA DELONEY

"Dang, baby. Can't I get a smile, a hug, something? You act like you're not happy to see a brother."

"I'm not. For the last time: What. Are. You. Doing. Here?"

He reached over to hug her, but she stepped back. "Oh, it's like that?" he asked.

"Yes, it's like that! You disappear without any explanation, without any warning. I see you on Facebook with your new boo. And now, after two years, you show up—unannounced—on my doorstep, and you act like I'm just supposed to welcome you back with open arms? You have lost your raggedy mind."

"Aw, come on, Bri. We had a good thing, you know that."

"Yes," Brianna replied, "we did. But you walked out on that. You walked out on me. I didn't hear a peep from you. Did you know I was in an accident last year? I could have died, and you wouldn't have known or cared."

He took another step toward the door. "I care, baby. I'm here. I want us again."

She held up her hand against his chest to stop his forward motion. "Not a chance. You need to go, right now."

She was so focused on Pete, she didn't notice Jake ambling up behind him until he spoke. "Is everything okay here, Brianna?"

Pete turned to face Jake. "Yo bruh, this is between me and my girl."

"I am not your girl. And I asked you to leave, Pete," Brianna said.

"C'mon, Bri, let's take this inside."

"No. Now go, please."

"The lady asked you to go, *bruh*," Jake warned. "I think you should do as she asked." In his hand, he held his badge and identification.

"Oh, it's like that? Aight, aight. I'm not tryin' to catch a case. I'll holla at you later, Bri." He gave Jake a menacing look before turning away from the house and walking away.

Brianna let out a long sigh and sagged against the doorway. "I am so sorry about that, Jake. I had no idea he was going to show up like that."

"I'm glad I was here then. Are you alright? If you don't feel up to going out, I understand. We could do this another time, if you're willing."

She shook her head. "No. I'm really glad you're here. And I'm looking forward to our date. But you have to tell me if I'm dressed appropriately." She spun around and he whistled appreciatively.

"You look fantastic. And yes, you're fine. I mean, you're dressed fine!" He shook his head. "Wow, I can't even believe I said that."

She grinned. "Are you going to tell me where we're going?"

He smiled back. "Nope. It's a surprise." He held out his hand. "Ready?"

She took it. "Ready."

CHAPTER ELEVEN

Jake led Brianna to his Chevy Tahoe and let her in. As they settled in to drive, he turned on the satellite radio to a smooth jazz station. Brianna nodded her approval. They were quiet at first, then Jake broke the ice. "Sooo… you want to tell me about ol' dude?"

Brianna rolled her eyes. "That was Peter Bradford. My long ago, long forgotten ex. I don't know how he had the nerve to show up at my house without so much as a call or a text."

"Is he violent?"

"No! Pete's never been violent with me."

"He looked a little aggressive. And a little high."

"You think he was high?"

"Possibly. I couldn't get a good read on him, but his eyes looked dilated."

She sighed again. "I don't know what he got into when he left me."

"Do you mind if I ask why he left?"

She shrugged. "To be honest, I don't know. I mean, we had been together for two years. We had our issues, you know, but all couples have those. If I had to really nail it down, we were unequally yoked."

"Spiritually?"

"Yes. He wanted to move in with me, and I wouldn't let him. The Holy Spirit convicted me about sleeping with him, so I cut him off. And I knew if he moved in, I wouldn't be able to do it. I was growing in the Lord; he was running away from Him. I guess I knew all along we weren't going to work out, but he was what I knew. And a part of me still loved him and wanted him."

"Now?"

She laughed. "Not a chance. I've moved on with my life, and there's no room for anyone that doesn't believe what I believe."

"Does that mean there's room for me?"

She ducked her head. "I know you're a believer. As for the rest, we'll see. Maybe if you tell me where we're going…"

He laughed. "You are slick, Brianna. But I am not telling you. You'll just have to be surprised."

***

Jake watched from a distance as Brianna sat staring at the word waterfall. He marveled at the graceful way she turned her head to read the quotes that appeared. He heard her breath catch at the images the light created with the words on the wall. He knew he had impressed her with the trip to the American Writers Museum. From the moment they walked in, Brianna was entranced. She was positively giddy when they entered the children's room. She regaled him with tales of the children's stories she had read as a child and the memories they conjured. There was nothing but delight on her face as she listened to Langston Hughes' voice reciting one of his poems.

At every exhibit, Brianna had something to share and marvel at. She laughed out loud when she saw the names of Prince and Tupac Shakur on the walls of the great American writing innovators listed among the likes of James Weldon Johnson and Maya Angelou.

But it was the word waterfall that had left her speechless. It felt like a sacred space. Jake stayed as motionless as he could. He didn't want to disturb her in her element. Moments later, she turned towards him, as if realizing he was still there. Her eyes were moist as she whispered, "That was beautiful."

"I'm glad you enjoyed it. But there's still more to see. Or not, up to you."

"Just give me a few minutes."

He nodded, then eased his way beside her. "It really is amazing. When you think of the creativity that went into creating this and then the technical side of it. Call me impressed."

"I know. It really makes the idea of words having life more powerful," Brianna said. She leaned into him and Jake felt his heart skip a beat feeling her closeness. After another minute, she stood. "Let's go see what else is there."

In the next exhibit, they laughed as they tried out the manual typewriters. Then they switched to the laptops where they were able to create their own stories. Brianna dove in, quickly typing out a short missive. Jake's hand hovered over the keyboard. He had no idea what to write. He finally hit on an idea and typed out a sentence. Brianna came around to see what he wrote. "Unh-unh," he said. "You first."

In the span of less than five minutes, Brianna had crafted a mini-short story about a mother-daughter tea party. It was brief, but sweet, and Jake swore he could imagine the entire story laid out. "Your turn," she said.

Jake sighed and turned his laptop around so she could read aloud. "The quick brown fox jumps over the lazy dog." She looked up at him quizzically. "That's all you wrote?"

"It was the only thing that came to mind. I remembered it from typing class in high school."

"You took a typing class?"

Jake nodded. "I had a crush on a girl. It was the only class I had that I could sit next to her and talk to her. I made a lot of mistakes, mostly to get her to help me."

"And did she?"

"She did. But outside of class, she ignored me. I think she thought I was stalking her."

"You were!"

"I was not. Not technically. Anyway, I passed the class—barely. But it helps me when I type up my reports. But look at you! You're the real writer here. Your story is really good."

She shrugged. "It's nothing. Just popped into my head."

"I've always admired writers, the way they seem to conjure something out of nothing. That's not my cup of tea."

"What is your cup of tea?"

"I need to work with what I can see. I need facts. I think that's why I enjoy law enforcement. I know the law; I understand the law. And I know how to deal with those who break the law, even if it's as simple as a speeding ticket."

"Is everything black and white with you?" Brianna asked.

"Not always. I use my judgment when I can. Like today with—what was his name?"

"Pete."

"Right, Pete. Technically, he was trespassing, and I suspected he was under the influence. I could have detained him and had him arrested."

"But you didn't."

"I didn't need to. Once he saw my badge, he walked away. That's all I needed him to do. Besides, I didn't want to spoil our date. Spending time with you was far more important to me than arresting some knucklehead."

Brianna blushed. "You made a wise choice, grasshopper. C'mon, let's finish seeing the rest of the museum."

They continued their tour of the museum, sharing their thoughts on the writers and the works they represented. At the end of the tour, Brianna excused herself to the restroom, while Jake made a pit stop at the gift shop. When she returned, he presented her with a gift: a coffee mug that made her laugh out loud.

"I love this," she exclaimed. She read off the caption: "Sometimes I'm content being a mild-mannered writer. Other times I think I should start unleashing my super powers." She looked over at him. "What if writing is my super power?"

"Nope, that's just one of them."

"What are the others?" she asked.

"I'm hoping to find out."

CHAPTER TWELVE

After the museum, they had a late lunch at Sweetwater Grille across the street from the museum. Brianna hated to admit it, but she was starving. She confessed it to Jake, who told her to order whatever she wanted. She ordered a barbeque bacon cheeseburger and fries and Jake did the same. Over their meal, they talked more about how they came to their respective professions.

"I was pre-law in college. Took my LSATs and got accepted into law school. When I graduated, I took the bar and passed, but I wasn't as convinced that I wanted to practice law. I felt God leading me towards more hands-on work. One weekend, I was hanging out with some friends playing basketball in the park. The police were patrolling the area like they always did. One of my boys began swearing at the cops, saying how they were profiling us because we were black. Bear in mind, the officers in the car were black! And they had done nothing or said anything to us. Suddenly we heard gunshots. We ran for cover as the police put on lights and sirens and headed in the direction of the shooting. Cops came from everywhere. I went over to where the action was. There was a young man bleeding in the street. I'd seen him in the neighborhood, but I didn't know him personally. The officers were trying to get information about who had shot the boy, but all the crowd was saying was 'Eff-this' and 'eff-you'. They wouldn't cooperate at all. And I thought, how are we ever going to build a bridge between the cops and the community without cooperation? I went home and filled out an application. CPD was going through changes and not enrolling in the academy. I applied to the Illinois State Police. The rest is history."

"That's pretty noble of you."

"Nothing noble about it. It's the truth as I saw it. As I see it. Tell me something. Why did you become a teacher?"

She smiled. "Someone has to do it."

"Seriously."

"Okay, seriously. I've always known somehow that I was going to be a teacher. We took these spiritual gifts assessments at church once. Mine turned out to be teacher. It made sense because I was always teaching at church or tutoring someone in school."

"But what about writing? It's clear you have a passion for it."

"I do enjoy it, true. I also love reading. But I'd never be able to make a living at it."

"How do you know?"

"Do you know how hard it is to get an agent, much less a publisher? Besides, the publishing landscape has changed so much. Unless you're J.K. Rowling or Steve Harvey, you'd have to have a large platform to get a publisher to take notice. I don't have the time to do all that."

"Have you thought about publishing it yourself? I hear there are a lot of writers going that route."

"I have, but I'm not sure if I'm ready for that yet."

"Will you let me be the judge?"

She shook her head. "I'm not ready for an audience, yet."

"When you are, will you let me read it?"

"I'll think about it."

They continued their conversation, lingering over dessert and coffee. When Jake's phone buzzed, he ignored it, engrossed in his time with Brianna. The second time it buzzed, he paused. "I'm sorry. Let me check this."

"Is that your girlfriend checking up on you? Or your boy giving you an excuse to end our date?"

"Ha-ha." He checked his phone, then frowned. "It looks I really do have to end our date." He saw Brianna's suspicious expression. "No, really. My buddy's wife went into early labor and I need to go in and cover his shift. I'm sorry, Brianna." He signaled the waiter for the check. "I was hoping we could get in a ride on the Ferris wheel at Navy Pier."

Brianna sighed. "It's okay. I can use the time to work on my manuscript."

***

The drive to Brianna's house was relatively quick. When they pulled up, she was about to open her door, when Jake stopped her. "Wait, please. Let me." He hopped out his side and ran over to her door and let her out. "I'll walk you to your door."

"You don't have to do that," she said.

"I know. I want to." He continued walking with her up to her door. As they stood in front of her door, Jake took her hand. "I had a really nice time, Brianna."

"So did I, Jake."

"Do you mind if I do something?"

"Something... like what?"

"This." He took her other hand in his and bowed his head. "Father, thank you for your mercy and grace and protection. Thank you for this wonderful day that we were able to spend together. Thank you for Brianna, your daughter. Thank you for heart, her spirit, her dedication, and her commitment to her students and to her writing. I pray you will protect and keep her through this night. In Jesus name I pray, Amen."

Brianna followed suit. "Thank you, Father, for my brother in Christ, Jake. Thank you for what you have done in his life, thank you for what you are doing and what you will do in, though, and for him. I pray he will always keep you first in his life. Protect him tonight as he goes to work and keep him and his fellow officers safe. I pray for his friend's wife, that all goes well with the delivery of their baby. Keep us and guide us. In Jesus' name I pray, Amen."

She looked up to see Jake grinning madly at her. "What?"

"You're the first woman I've dated that prayed with me openly on our first date."

"You're the first that prayed at all on the first date."

"I'm glad I was your first." They both laughed at the irony of his words. "I should go. May I call later if it's not too late?"

"Yes, please. I'll be up until 11:00."

He nodded then leaned in and kissed her on the cheek. "That's something else I've wanted to do all night." He released her hands then turned to head back to his truck. He stopped and turned back to say, "Say hello to Liz for me."

Brianna laughed as she went inside the door.

CHAPTER THIRTEEN

"I cannot believe that *pendejo* had the nerve to show up at your house!" Liz exclaimed. She rocked Bella in her arms as the two women sat in the fellowship hall after Sunday morning worship service.

"Watch your mouth, Liz," Brianna said, laughing. "You're in church. And you're holding your daughter."

"She doesn't understand yet, but I will teach her. Did he say what he wanted?"

"Nope, and I could care less. I just want him to disappear like he did two years ago."

"You and Jake, huh? Luis was right about the two of you. You sound like you had a great time."

"We really did. The museum is amazing. We have to plan a field trip there soon. It was a great idea; I'll have to thank Luis."

"Thank me for what?" Luis asked, sidling up to his wife.

"For telling Jake all my secrets."

"What secrets? What, that you have dreams of becoming the next Pearl Cleage or Terry McMillan?" he asked.

"More like Reshonda Tate Billingsley. I loved that movie they did from her book. Do you think I could get Ava DuVernay to direct my movie?"

"Only if you finish your book and get it published," Liz replied. "You've been sitting on it for far too long. As soon as you get it done, I'm going to send it to Oprah. She'll make the movie."

"From your mouth to God's ear."

"Jake said he had a fantastic time," Luis said. "I'm glad it's working out for you two."

"Whoa, big papa. I'm not sure this is going anywhere yet."

"What do you mean?" Liz asked. "What's the problem? He's fine, he's saved, he's a gentleman and he's gainfully employed."

"That's the problem. His choice of employment."

"He's a police officer. What's wrong with that?" Luis said.

"Not this again," Liz said, shaking her head.

"I just don't think it's a good idea to get involved with a cop, even if he's a state trooper," Brianna said.

"Let me ask you this: if he were a teacher, a plumber, or a garbage man, and he had all the same qualities that you like, would you continue to see him?" Liz asked.

"Maybe. Probably, yes."

"You're saying the only thing wrong with him is his choice of profession."

"Yes."

"Why? What are you afraid of?"

Brianna flashed back to the day of the accident. It was Jake who had shown up, who had helped everyone escape the wreckage. It was in Jake's arms that she collapsed. And though she had stopped blaming him for Ron's death, there was a part of her that couldn't comprehend how he could risk his life for complete strangers. It was a fear she couldn't address out loud. "I don't know," she finally said. "I just don't want to start something with him and it not work out."

"I don't know what's going on in your head, Bri," Luis said, "but I know you're letting fear rule your decisions. That's not like you."

"I agree," Liz said. "Maybe God sent him your way and you're allowing the enemy to push him out of your life. Have you prayed about it?"

Brianna shook her head. "Not yet. I mean, I've prayed, but not about building a relationship."

"I think it's about time, don't you?"

Luis added, "Jake and I have been praying about this potential relationship for a while now. Why don't you and Liz do the same and see what God says?"

"Y'all just aren't gonna quit, are you?" Brianna said, laughing.

"Nope," Liz replied. "Give him a chance. Let's pray on it and if God says no, then we'll both shut up. Deal?"

"Deal."

CHAPTER FOURTEEN

The knot in Brianna's stomach grew as the clock ticked toward 8:00 p.m. She knew Jake was about to call and she wasn't sure she would answer. Despite her earlier promise to Liz and Luis, she knew the best thing would be to break up with Jake before either of them became seriously vested in a relationship. Yet, the thought of ending things before they had a chance to really grow didn't sit well with her. "Father," she prayed, "I don't know what to do. I don't know if Jake is meant for me. I just know I can't shake this fear in my heart. And I don't want to hurt him. Please, please, help me."

The phone rang, jarring her out of her contemplative words. Without even checking the caller ID, she answered. "Hi Jake."

"Jake, huh?" Pete responded. "What kind of janky name is that?"

"Why are you calling me, Pete? You lost my number once. Do it again."

"Now why you gotta be like that, babe? You know you miss me."

"No, Pete, I don't. Once upon a time, I missed you, or rather, I missed what I thought we might become. But I'm so far over you. I can't believe you have the nerve to even call me, much less show up at my door! Don't you ever show up like that again, understand?"

"Yeah, okay, that wasn't cool," Pete said. "But tell the truth, you know you were glad to see me, even a little bit."

"What do you want, Pete? I'm expecting a call."

"From Jake?"

"Not that it's any of your business, but yes, from him." She heard the beep and saw Jake's number come up. "That's him now."

"Wait, wait, wait—call me back!"

"Not a chance." She quickly switched over to her second call. "Hi."

"You okay?" Jake asked.

She sighed. "Pete was on the other line. I don't know what part of 'leave me alone' he does not get."

"Why did you answer his call?"

"I wasn't looking at the caller ID. I just assumed it was you."

"I'm sorry it wasn't."

"Me too." She sighed again. "As much as I am relieved to hear your voice…"

"Something else is bothering you. Talk to me."

"I don't know how to say this," she began. She could feel tears welling up in her eyes. "I don't think this is a good idea."

"What?"

"You. Me. Us. I don't think we should see each other again."

"Wait, where is this coming from? Did I do something wrong?"

"No. It's not you, it's me." She laughed at the tired cliché. "If I wrote that in my story, I'd smack myself."

"Does this have anything to do with Pete?"

"Lord, no!"

"Then what is it, really?"

"I just... I don't know..."

"Are you busy?"

"Right now? No, why?"

"I know it's a little late for Sunday night, but can I come over? Just to talk? I think we have something good here. Before we kill it, at least talk to me face to face. After we talk, if you're still ready to end things, I'll respect that. Please?"

She didn't know why, but she felt at ease. "Okay."

"I'll be there in fifteen minutes."

CHAPTER FIFTEEN

Exactly fifteen minutes later, Jake was at Brianna's doorstep. He took a few deep breaths before ringing her door. He'd been driving home when they talked, but as soon as she said she wanted to end things, he made a U-turn towards her townhouse. He didn't know what he was going to do if she told him not to come over; he was glad when she agreed to see him.

He was falling in love with Brianna. He wasn't sure when it happened, but he knew how he felt. He had been praying for her constantly and believed in his heart that God had sanctioned this relationship from the beginning. He had to get to the bottom of what was troubling her.

When she opened the door, it was all Jake could do not to pull her in his arms and kiss her. She had her shoulder length curls pulled up into a clip, with just a few hanging around her face. She'd removed any trace of makeup, with the exception of a hint of a burgundy lipstick. She had on a loose-fitting tee and leggings that showed off her lovely curves. "Are you sure it's okay that I came over?"

"I wouldn't have said so if it wasn't," she replied, smiling. He wanted to trace his fingers in the deep dimples of her cheeks. For a moment, he imagined what it would be like to caress her body…

"Jake?"

"Mmm."

She waved a hand in his face. "Are you just going to stand there all night?"

"Oh, yeah. Right." He coughed, trying to bring his mind back to his original purpose. He entered the living room and took a look around. The bookshelves in the corner were lined with assorted novels, writing reference books and biblical resources. On another shelf, she had DVDs. He was surprised that the collection included many black and white films from the 30s, 40s and 50s.

"I love the dialogue in these," Brianna said, coming along side of him. "The actors make it work, but they have great material to work with. A lot of today's movies get lost in loud music, special effects, or actors over-acting. The best movies are the ones that lose you in the words."

He pulled one of the DVDs from the shelf. "The Thin Man?" he quizzed.

"Have you seen it? William Powell and Myrna Loy are one of the best comedy teams on the planet. The dialogue crackles so fast in these films. It forces you to pay attention even as you're laughing and trying to figure out the mystery."

"I'm more of a Scorsese fan," Jake said. "He is a fantastic director."

"Yes, but so many of his films are violent," she replied

"Are you a Tyler Perry fan?" he asked.

"I am. His films aren't perfect, and I know folks get down on him for dressing in drag as Madea. But they didn't say that about Flip Wilson or Martin Lawrence. Tyler's movies have a heart and a message."

"What do you know about Flip Wilson?"

"YouTube." She stopped to look at him plainly. "I know you didn't come here to discuss my tastes in movies and TV."

"You're right I didn't. When I called, you sounded upset. And when you said you wanted to end things—"

"I meant what I said, Jake."

"Okay. But at least tell me why, and maybe give me a chance to change your mind.

She rolled her eyes and sighed. "Would you like a cup of coffee?"

"Sure. Decaf if you have it. Black, please."

As she made her way to the kitchen, he looked around more. There were a few photos of her with her family, Liz and Luis and some with her students. There were a few decorative wall sculptures of encouraging words: faith, love, hope, and family. She had a desk in the corner, which contained her laptop, iPad, and several notepads. "You write longhand? I'd have thought you were digitally inclined."

She returned with two mugs in her hand and handed him one. "I like the feel of writing. It's very freeing. The laptop can become a distraction, what with the internet, games, and email. And I can always pull out a notebook or my iPad Pro wherever I am, but it's not always convenient to pull out my laptop. Like if I'm at church and I get a thought, I can quickly jot down the note. It would be rather awkward to use my laptop in the choir stand."

"You sing?"

"Yes, but I'm not a soloist. I'm definitely a background singer." She gestured for him to sit. "Jake, I didn't mean to be so abrupt on the phone, but I meant what I said. I don't think us seeing each other is a great idea."

"Why not?"

"I..." She tried to gather her thoughts. "You're a terrific guy. Considerate, kind, and you make me laugh."

"All perfectly reasonable traits that you don't want in a man," Jake said, with a chuckle.

The smile returned. "Exactly." The smile disappeared. "Can I be honest?"

"Please."

"Do you remember when we met?"

"Of course."

"You showed up and you were ready to head into that bus. I remember begging you to let me back in. You stopped me."

"You're not still mad about that, are you?"

"No! What scares me is that you were fully prepared to go into that bus, weren't you."

"Yes."

"Despite the fact that the bus was on fire."

"Yes. You said there was someone still in there. If the firefighters hadn't arrived when they did, I would have gone in."

"You could have died."

"Possibly."

"You say that so nonchalantly."

"Don't mistake my tone. I take life and death very seriously. I have to, because it's my job. I knew when I signed up that wearing the badge automatically put a target on my back. And it also means that sometimes I have to put my life on the line. The reality is, I may not live through my shift. If I can't live with that, I have no business being a cop. But what gives me strength, what gives me peace, what gives me courage to put on my badge and do my job, is my faith in Jesus Christ. I know where my soul will spend eternity."

She shook her head. "I don't know if I can deal with that."

"Listen, you know as well as I do that you are not guaranteed any time except the moment we are living in. You know there's no real safe place anymore. You're a teacher. You've seen the school shootings in the news. Does that stop you from doing your job?"

She shuddered at the memories. She fought back tears when she thought of the casualties in Newtown, Connecticut. *Those poor babies. Those poor families.* "No. But the chances of a shooting happening in school are next to zero compared to your job. You don't just have to worry about bullets. You could be in a crash, or some perp could shank you."

He laughed. "You've been watching too much television. Yes, those are real possibilities. But I don't dwell on that. Most days are uneventful. Maybe a speeding ticket or an arrest here and there."

"And the occasional bus crash, right?"

"Yeah. Let me ask you this: if I weren't a cop, would you go out with me?"

"I suppose."

"Okay. Let's do this. Let's just spend some time getting to know each other. Go out a few times, have some laughs. We don't have to talk about my job. If, after a while, you still can't get used to the idea of dating me–badge and all–we'll say goodbye and part as friends. Deal?" He held up his mug to toast.

She paused, then clinked his mug. "Deal."

CHAPTER SIXTEEN

On Monday near the end of third period, Brianna's phone buzzed with a text from the school office. "You have a visitor," it said.

She quickly typed, "Who is it?"

"He wouldn't give his name. He wants to surprise you," came the response.

Odd. It couldn't have been a parent; those meetings were usually scheduled for after school and in advance. The office administrator didn't typically play such games. Every visitor had to be logged in and escorted to their destination during school hours. Then it hit her: it has to be Jake. He had been to the school previously, and if he's in uniform, he wouldn't necessarily raise the suspicions of the office staff.

The bell sounded and her students quickly wrapped up their belongings to head to their next class. Brianna's next two periods were free. If Jake wanted to grab a quick lunch, she was more than willing. She waited until the second bell sounded before grabbing her purse and walking to the office. With the halls cleared, she started humming a Jill Scott tune and doing a little dance. She stopped herself. *Girl, get a grip. It's just lunch.*

Her good mood turned sour when she noticed the shoulder-length dreads on the man standing in the office. She let out a frustrated breath. Pete.

She opened the office door and he turned. For a moment, Brianna was caught breathless. She hadn't noticed the other day, but Pete had slimmed down but put on some muscle. She could she his well-defined torso and muscular arms under the long-sleeve cotton V-neck sweater he was wearing. His trousers were tailored and his shoes shined. He had trimmed his goatee to frame his gorgeous smile. His dreads were fresh and neat. On the outside, Pete was fabulous. Brianna knew what lurked inside. He held a bouquet of multi-colored sunflowers, which he held out to her. "Hi Brianna. I'm sorry about the whole surprise thing." He pushed the flowers towards her. "I remember how much you loved fresh cut flowers. I thought roses would be too much. But you could keep these in your classroom or at home in your office."

Brianna noticed the curious glances her way. She took the flowers and muttered a thank you, before grabbing his arm and leading him out of the office.

"He'll need a visitor's badge, Miss Norwood," the administrator called out.

"He's not staying," Brianna replied through gritted teeth. She followed Pete out the door and headed for the exit. Once safely outside of anyone's vision, Brianna whirled on him. "What are you doing here, Pete? First, you show up at my house and now you show up on my job? What part of I never want to see you again are you not getting? Do I need to get a restraining order? "

Pete threw up his hands. "Whoa, Bri, slow your roll. It's not like that. I just wanted to see if you'd talk to me. I tried to tell you that last night, but you hung up on me. I didn't want to take a chance at coming by the house again in case Barney Fife was hanging around."

She could feel her blood pressure rising. "What. Do. You. Want?"

"I just want to have a conversation with you, maybe over a cup of coffee. Ten minutes, maybe five. I have some things I want to tell you and I imagine there are more than a few things you want to say to me. Please, Bri. I wouldn't have come if it wasn't important."

Brianna stared into his eyes—those gorgeous brown eyes that had made her swoon from the first time they met. This time, they were filled with—sincerity, regret, desperation? She sighed. "Ten minutes and you promise to disappear and stay gone?"

"Yes, if that's what you want."

"I'll meet you at 4:00 at the café."

"I'll see you then."

***

The Southside Café was more like a dive than a café. Situated just off the expressway, it was one of those places Brianna ignored as she traveled back and forth. Early in their relationship, Pete had brought Brianna there on one of their dates. Internally, she was insulted, but she was won over by the delicious food and generous portions. She and Pete often returned to the café for a quick lunch or dinner.

The cashier greeted her warmly upon entering. She remembered Brianna from her previous visits. "It's been a long time. How ya been, sweetie?"

Brianna smiled. "I'm good."

"Your fella's in your booth."

"Thanks," Brianna said, inwardly rolling her eyes. The idea that anyone still thought of Pete as her "fella" made her stomach churn. Pete stood as she approached and waited for her to be seated.

"I'm glad you came, Bri," Pete said. "I thought you'd get a kick out of sitting in our old spot. Do you want to order something?"

"No. You said you wanted to talk. Talk."

He nodded. "That's one of the things I love about you, Bri. Straight shooter." He glanced up as the waitress brought over a slice of French silk pie and a cup of coffee and sat it in front of Brianna. "I ordered it because I remembered it was your favorite afternoon treat."

Brianna waited until the waitress left before shoving the food over to Pete. "I'm not hungry. Say what you want to say. I've got work to do."

"Okay. Well... the thing is... I want to apologize."

"Apologize for what?"

"For everything. I want to apologize for the way I acted towards the end, for walking out on you, for disappearing without saying goodbye. It was a childish way to handle things and I know I hurt you deeply. I apologize, Bri. I'm sorry for it all. I hope you can forgive me."

Brianna leaned back into seat. "Why Pete? Why now? You've been gone two years and in all that time, you could have said the same things. Did you know I nearly died last year in an accident?"

"I think you mentioned that before. What happened?"

"It was a school bus accident. Driver going the wrong way plowed into our bus. It was in the news for a while."

"I think I remember that story. That was you?"

"Yes."

"But you're okay?"

"Yes, I'm fine, thank the Lord."

"Amen." He took a forkful of the pie and shoved it into his mouth. "Mmmm… this is delicious. You sure you don't want any?"

"I'm fine. You haven't answered my question."

"What question?"

"Why did you wait until now to apologize?"

He shrugged. "Long story short, I was a boy. I thought like a boy. I acted like a boy. I didn't understand what you were trying to do. But I've grown up. And I understand things a little clearer now. You weren't rejecting me. You were convinced that the only way we were going to get married is if you cut me off."

She shook her head. "No, Pete, that's not what I was trying to do. I was growing in my relationship with the Lord and I was convicted about my behavior. Sleeping with you was outside the will of God. I wanted us to be in His will. You weren't ready to hear that."

"You're right. I wasn't ready then. I'm ready now."

"Ready for what?"

"To listen. To start over again. To give us another chance. You have to admit, things between us were pretty good. I miss you, Bri.

I miss us." He reached across and took her hand in his. "I'd like another chance to prove I'm worthy of you. Will you at least consider it?"

Brianna eased her hand from his. She took slow, measured breaths to calm the electricity sparking in her. Without a doubt, she and Pete always had great chemistry. Two years apart had not changed anything. "I need to get home, Pete."

"Can I call you later?"

She nodded then rose and headed out the door.

CHAPTER SEVENTEEN

One week later, Brianna's heart was overflowing with joy. Sunday morning, Luis and Elizabeth were celebrating baby Isabella's dedication and Brianna and Luis' brother, Ronaldo, were being officially named the baby's godparents. Bella's grandmothers had been cooking all weekend and there was to be a grand feast at the house after the service. Luis mentioned that Jake would be joining them as soon as he got off work.

Brianna hadn't seen Jake all week, as his shift switched to evenings to cover for another sergeant who was on vacation. They had spoken frequently through the week, though Brianna never mentioned her conversation with Pete.

On the other hand, Pete had made his presence known. He had an Edible Arrangement sent to her job. They had a pleasant dinner at the café. When he noticed her tire was a little low, he offered to have it checked and repaired while she was at work. It was those kinds of niceties that made Brianna fall in love with him in the first place.

Brianna was confused. Her feelings for Jake were growing, but so were her feelings for Pete. What's worse, she felt like she couldn't say anything to anyone. She'd tried to pray on the situation, but she wasn't getting any guidance from the Lord.

She refocused her attention on the service and rocking Bella, who was drifting off to sleep. The minister in the pulpit asked for all the visitors to stand. Brianna turned around, hoping to see Jake. Instead, she gasped: Pete was standing up in the rear of the sanctuary. She whirled back around, jostling Bella, who let out a quick cry, but quickly settled down. Leaning over to Liz, she whispered, "Oh my God, Pete's here!"

"What?" Liz whipped around in her seat and scanned the crowd. She turned back around. "What is he doing here? Did you know he was coming?"

"No! I had no idea. Oh man, if he's here and Jake sees him..."

"What's the big deal? Jake won't start anything in church. I hope Pete has better sense than that."

"It's just the last time the two of them saw each other, it wasn't pretty."

"Why did he show up today of all days?" Liz asked.

Brianna glanced down at the sleeping baby. "I kinda told him about the blessing."

Liz frowned. "You 'kinda' told him? You've been talking to him."

"Yes, a little. Look, it's a long story, and now's not the time to get into it."

"Indeed. We'll talk this afternoon. Apparently, you've been holding out on me."

"Shhh... the pastor is speaking."

***

At the conclusion of the service, the pastor called for all the families of the children who were being dedicated to come down to the altar. Brianna stood and handed Bella over to her parents. She and Ronaldo followed them, along with the rest of the family. As they reached the front, she heard the clicking of a camera next to her. She turned to see Jake holding his camera. "When did you get here?" she whispered.

"During the sermon. I sat in the back so I wouldn't disturb. I promised Luis I'd take some pictures." He held up the camera and snapped one of her.

"I think you're supposed to be photographing Bella," she said, grinning.

"Yes, but I'm also supposed to focus on her godparents too, right?"

Brianna shook her head as Jake turned to focus on the baby. He began snapping away as Luis handed Bella to one of the ministers, who took her on stage with the other babies being blessed. Bella, who had napped during the service, was wide awake and smiling her toothless grin. Jake took several pictures, pausing only when the pastor began to pray over the babies. He resumed snapping as soon as the prayer was over and the benediction was given. The minister returned Bella to Luis and Jake began snapping pictures of the family, then more with Bella and Ronaldo holding their goddaughter.

It was a joyous time until Bella began crying. "She's probably hungry," Liz declared, fishing in the diaper bag for a bottle. She handed it off to Brianna, who gave it to the baby, who eagerly sucked it down. Brianna rocked the baby as she gave her the bottle.

She didn't notice Pete sidling up to her, until he said, "That's a good look on you." Before she had a chance to respond, he walked over to Luis and shook his hand. "Hey man, congrats on your beautiful little girl."

Luis shook his hand and thanked him. "Haven't seen you in a minute, Pete. How you been?"

"I'm good man, I'm good." He leaned over to give Liz a kiss on her cheek, which she reluctantly accepted. "I see she gets her good looks from you."

"I'm surprised to see you here, Pete," Liz responded tersely.

"Yeah, well, I'm full of surprises, right Bri?"

Brianna glanced up to see Jake giving her a curious look. "Ah, Pete, you remember Jake Lewis. Jake, this is Peter Bradford."

"We've met," Jake said extending his hand. "Good to see you again, *bruh*."

"Likewise, sheriff," Pete replied, a tinge of sarcasm in his voice. He turned back to Brianna. "Hey, I was wondering if you had plans this afternoon. I wanted to continue our conversation from the other night."

"Um, well… We're heading over to Luis and Liz's to celebrate the baby's blessing."

"You're welcome to come join us," Luis said, ignoring the daggers Liz and Brianna were shooting his way. "There's plenty of food and always room for one more."

"Nah, I'm good," Pete responded. "I don't want to intrude on a family event. Bri, I'll call you later, okay?" He turned and left.

"Yeah, sure," she muttered. She turned her attention back to the baby, ignoring Jake's curious gaze. "I think she needs a change." She reached for the diaper bag.

"I'll go with you," Liz said, smacking Luis in the arm hard.

"What was that for?" he yelped.

Liz responded by swearing at him in Spanish. Liz's mother, Julia, yelled, "Not in church, Elizabeth!"

CHAPTER EIGHTEEN

At the Trujillo's home, Brianna jumped right in with the celebration. A frequent guest of the family, she didn't hesitate to help the elder women with setting out the food and arranging the seating. Part of it was because she genuinely enjoyed helping out, but mostly it was because she was busy trying to avoid Jake, who seemed to be following her everywhere she went.

When she finally sat down to eat, Jake pulled up a seat in front of her. "What a day," he said. "Such a beautiful celebration of life and moving forward, don't you think?"

"Yes," Brianna replied. She shoved the food on her plate around with a fork. "It was nice."

He grabbed her fork hand to stop its motion. "Brianna, look at me, please." She looked up slowly, but did not speak. "One of the things you should know about me is that I don't like playing games, unless they're actually, you know, games. I'm a pretty straight shooter, no pun intended, and anyone that I'm involved with needs to be the same with me." When she didn't respond, he asked, "Are you going to tell me what's going on with you and Pete?"

She shrugged. "There's nothing going on. Not really."

"What does 'not really' mean?"

Sighing, she replied, "We went out for coffee to talk. He apologized for how he left things between us. He said he's grown up and he wants us to be friends."

"Friends. I see. So when your 'friend' showed up today, you looked like you were ready to crawl under the pew."

"I didn't know he was coming, I swear."

"If you're just friends, why were you acting so awkward? And why have you been ducking me all afternoon?"

"I don't know, Jake. It's complicated."

"You said you went out for coffee. Nothing more?"

"No. Well, we have been talking on the phone. And he sent me flowers at work. I gave them to the office administrator."

Jake nodded. "Do you have feelings for him?"

She opened her mouth and closed it. She sighed again. "I don't know. I'm just trying to figure it all out."

"I see. And what about us? Do I factor in your feelings?"

"Yes, of course you do. I care about you very much, Jake."

"But a part of you still wants to be with him."

"I'd be lying if I said no. I've been praying, asking God to help me figure it all out."

"And?"

"Nothing. It's like he's gone silent."

"Or maybe you're not listening. One thing I know about the Lord is this: he's not going to superimpose his will over yours. But he will give you clear direction if you truly seek it. In my opinion, you don't really want to know what God thinks. You want what's easy and familiar. Pete broke your heart and for whatever reason, he's trying to worm his way back into your life. I think you know the right thing to do. If you're praying for discernment, he'll show it to you, if you're ready to receive."

Brianna felt herself growing warm. "Oh, now I'm not spiritual enough, is that what you're saying?"

"Nope, not at all. What I am saying is that I'm going to remove myself from the equation. If he's whom you want to be with and God grants you peace, then go for it. I won't be a stumbling block for you. But if you decide it's me you want to be with, let me know." He leaned in and gave her a soft kiss on the lips. "I'm gonna say goodbye to our hosts."

CHAPTER NINETEEN

For the most part, Brianna spent the week in a funk. Each day she went to work on automatic pilot. She plastered a smile on her face and greeted everyone. She had coffee with Liz, but she always cut it short, citing other duties needing her attention. She was curt with her students, getting frustrated when they seemed to be lacking focus on their assignments.

Wednesday night, she skipped out on Bible class and instead turned on the TV. It seemed everything that was on was romantic in nature, except for the standard woman-in-jeopardy flicks. She hated those. She turned off the TV and grabbed her laptop Opening up her current work in progress, she stared at the screen, waiting for the next inspiration to hit. After ten minutes, she closed it out and grabbed her notebook and a pen. *I need to free write.* It was a technique that she taught her students to use when they had to work on an essay or another assignment. It was a great way to get the class focused.

This is ridiculous, she began writing. *I don't know what's wrong with me. I can't seem to focus on anything and I feel all alone. Well, that's my choice. I shut the door on Jake and Pete has been bugging the crap outta me all week. Ugh. I mean, I'm trying to be friends, but he keeps pushing for more. More what? More of me? Of us? Of what we used to be? Is that what I want? What do I want? Who do I want? Why did Jake say I wasn't asking for clear direction? I mean, I've been praying and asking God and I don't understand why he doesn't just come out and say it. It's not like I'm asking for something big. Or maybe I am. Maybe I'm just scared of opening my heart. Maybe I'm just not ready to commit. Or maybe I just don't know if I can commit to either one of these guys. What would that mean–to commit? Marriage? Kids? I want that, but do I want that with Pete? Or Jake? I used to want that with Pete. I did. Why am I not so sure now? And what about Jake? What would it mean to be committed to him? Can I really see myself married to a police officer? What if he's catastrophically injured on the job? Am I ready to take care of an invalid for the rest of my life? Or what if he's killed? Do I want to be a widow? I'm too young to wear black all the time. Despite what others say, it doesn't look all that slimming on someone my size. Just because I don't look like a pumpkin doesn't mean I'm not a giant acorn.*

She slammed the notebook closed. "This is getting me nowhere," she muttered. She had hoped the free write session would unblock her so she could write. Instead, it had merely given a solid voice to the thoughts swirling around in her head. She had to talk to someone objective.

****

"Hey baby girl!" Ernest Norwood's deep baritone echoed through the phone. "I thought you'd be at church tonight."

"Hi Daddy," Brianna answered. Her father knew her so well. "I wasn't feeling well, so I thought I'd stay home and rest up. Plus, we haven't talked in a while. I miss you, Daddy."

Ernest chuckled. "I'm not dead, baby girl. And if you miss me, you could always hop a plane and come see us."

"Ha! Between your mission trips and your vacations, you're never home long enough for a visit. I'm actually surprised to catch you at home."

"Well, your mother and I decided to put a hold on traveling for a while. It's such a pain to get through the airport these days. And she's having issues with her knees, which makes walking difficult for her. The doctor wants to do a knee replacement, but your mother is having none of that."

"Tell mom to stop being difficult. If having the knee replacement done will help her, she should do it!"

"You tell her. She can yell at you then and leave me alone." He laughed and Brianna joined in. "Alright, Miss Bri. We've had our laugh for the day. The last time I got a call from you in the middle of the week, you were laid up in the hospital after the accident. You're all right, aren't you?"

"I'm fine, Dad. Physically, anyway. Emotionally, well that's a different story." She proceeded to share with her father the details of her aborted relationship with Jake and the reemergence of Pete in her life. "I've been praying about this, Dad. I have. Jake said if I really wanted a clear answer, I'd have one."

"Sounds like a good guy to me, though I haven't given him my fatherly once-over," Ernest said. A former deacon, he had drilled every guy Brianna had been in a serious relationship since college.

"You know how I feel about Pete. I wasn't on board with the two of you in the first place. He was leading you down a dark path and once you opened your eyes to the truth, he rabbited."

"Yes, I know, Dad, I was there. He's apologized for that and I think he's really sincere. He seems to have changed."

"Why? Because he took you to your favorite joint? Because he brought you flowers? He showed up at church? What about him has changed?"

"I think he's changed. He seems more thoughtful when we talk. He sounds sincere in his words."

"Listen to yourself, hon: you *think* he's changed. He *seems*, he *sounds*. You're not even sure yourself if he's for real or not."

"We're just taking it slow, trying to get to know each other again."

"Tell me about Jake."

The abrupt turn in the conversation threw her off. "Um… he's, he's kind, sweet, handsome, funny. He loves the Lord. On our first date, he asked me to pray with him. He's a gentleman."

Ernest chuckled. "You should hear how you sound when you talk about him. There's a sweetness in your voice, a confidence, that I don't hear and have never heard when you've talked about Pete."

"Really?"

"Yes, really. Honey, I think you have your answer, but you don't want to accept it. Why are you hesitating when it comes to Jake? He sounds like everything you've ever wanted in a man."

"Except for his job. Daddy, I don't know if I can be in a relationship with someone who could get killed on their job."

"Bri, in this day and age, no one is safe on their job. Every time I hear of a school shooting, I pray that it's not yours. You know the

Bible says our days are not promised to us. Jake could die of a heart attack before he gets shot. You could develop a brain tumor and die before he does."

"Daddy!"

"I'm just saying! Look, I don't know if Jake is the one for you. But if you live your life in fear of the unknown, you will always live in fear. That's not what we want for you. That's not what God wants for you. Remember Jeremiah 29:11."

Brianna quoted the familiar passage. "For I know the plans I have for you, declares the Lord, plans for your welfare and not for evil, to give you a future and a hope."

"Exactly. You have to know that whoever God wants for you, he's going to be someone who wants the best for you. He's going to be someone who will encourage you, support you, and help you pursue your dreams and your destiny. He's going to be someone who will sacrifice himself to make sure you have everything you want or need. And when he finds you, you'll feel the same way."

Brianna wiped away a tear. "What if they both act like that? How will I know the difference?"

"In your heart, I think you already do. Matthew 7:15 and 16 says, 'Beware of false prophets who come to you in sheep's clothing but inwardly are ravenous wolves. You will recognize them by their fruits.' Baby, I think your prayer shouldn't be which one is right for you. I think your prayer should be let their real character reveal itself. Once you see it, you'll know who the right one is for you."

CHAPTER TWENTY

The next day over her lunch hour, Brianna called Jake. She was disappointed when she got his voicemail. "This is Jake. Please leave a message and I'll return your call as soon as possible. Thanks, and may God bless and keep you." At the beep, Brianna said, "Hi Jake. It's Brianna. I just called to say hi. I hope you are well. That's all. Oh, I miss you. Take care. Bye."

To her own ears, the message sounded weak and trifling. *But that's what I am. That's what I've become: weak and trifling. Maybe Daddy was right. Maybe I need to pray like he suggested.* The bell rang and she knew her students would be pouring into the classroom momentarily. She threw off a quick prayer: *Lord, let the real man stand up and the wrong one show himself.*

As the class began to settle in, her phone buzzed with a text from Pete: "Hey beautiful. Hope you're having a spectacular day. Dinner at your place tonight? I'm cooking. Love ya." She dashed off a quick response, then turned her attention to her students and the lesson at hand.

***

At 6:30 p.m., a grinning Pete arrived on Brianna's doorstep with a couple of bags of groceries. "I had to make sure I had the right ingredients for our dinner."

"What's in the bags?" she inquired, trying to peek inside. Pete brushed her aside.

"No, no, my lady. It's for me to know and you to find out." He went into the kitchen and set the bags on the counter. He began searching her cabinets and pulled out two wine glasses. The first thing he pulled out of the bag was a bottle of chardonnay. He uncorked the bottle and poured her a glass. "Nicely chilled for our dinner."

"Pete, you know I don't drink on a school night."

"Yes, I know. But today is Thursday and I know you have a shorter day on Friday. It's just one glass. You can sip on it all through dinner if you like. I just thought it would be a great way to relax you."

She reluctantly took the glass he offered and took a sip. "Mmm… this is nice."

"See? Now you sit back and let me get to work. Why don't you do some writing, unless you've got other work to do." He turned on her Bose system and connected his phone to an old school R&B station. As he worked, Pete began humming and dancing along to the music. Brianna smiled, watching him work. She couldn't remember seeing him so relaxed. "What are you cooking?"

"One of your favorite dishes: chicken fettuccine alfredo with spinach. I also have garlic bread and to top it off, chocolate cake and ice cream."

"Oh man, Pete. You're trying to kill me."

"I'm trying to love on you, woman." His phone rang and he checked it. "Let me just take this. I'll be right back." He scurried down the hall to the bathroom. He was back in three minutes. "Miss me?"

"You weren't gone that long. What was that all about?"

"Nothing. It was nothing. Let me get back to my business—dinner and you. How was your day?"

She began to share parts of her day. Pete seemed to be listening, but every once in a while, his phone would buzz. He'd stop and check, send a quick text, then resume what he was doing. It began happening more and more frequently, to the point where Brianna asked, "Pete, what's going on? Who's blowing up your phone?"

"I told you, baby, it's nothing. It's just a guy I know from back in the day. He has a business opportunity and he's trying to sell me on it."

"What's the business?"

"It's one of those multi-level marketing things. I'm not even trying to go there. He just won't quit though. Guess he's trying to make his monthly quota."

"Ugh, I know that feeling."

He slid the garlic bread in the oven. "Listen, don't worry about any of that. Sip your wine. Talk to me about your book. How's that going?"

"Double-ugh. Slow. Can't seem to get my mind focused."

"What are you writing? Fiction or non-fiction?"

"It's fiction. It's supposed to be young adult, you know, something my kids would read."

"What's it about?"

"Well, I based it on the Ten Commandments. It's supposed to be a series. The first one is based on Exodus 20:3: 'You shall have no other gods before me.'"

"Yikes. How does that work for kids?"

Internally, she flinched at his words. "Well, I have this set in a high school. Each book focuses on a specific student among this group of friends. The first one is a football player. His entire life is about football, to the point where he begins neglecting his studies, his friends and his relationship with God. When he makes football his god, he suffers the consequences."

"That's kind of a downer, isn't it?"

"Not exactly. Yes, he goes through something, but there is redemption for him in the end. All of the books are about redemption."

"Well, that's better. Can I top off your glass?"

"I'm fine, thanks. What about you, Pete? We're always talking about me. I want to know you."

"You know me, same ol', same ol'. I get up, go to work, and go home. The best part of my day is when I get to see you. Seeing you and I know my world is all right."

"What about church? What about your relationship with Christ?" Brianna asked

"I'm working on it and he's working on me. It's a work in progress, you know?" Pete replied.

"I know." She took a sniff. "I think the bread is ready."

He checked the oven. "You're right, it is. Dinner is served."

CHAPTER TWENTY-ONE

Pete plated the food and joined Brianna at the dining room table. He reached over to the counter and grabbed the bottle of chardonnay and set it on the table. He was about to dig in when Brianna reached over and took his hand. "Aren't you going to bless the food?"

He laughed. "You're right, I'm sorry. He bowed his head. "Good food, good meat, good God, let's eat!" He let out a laugh

Brianna smiled, but she felt a check in her spirit. *He's just trying to be funny.* She said her own prayer silently and began to eat. "Oh Pete, this is delicious! I forgot what a good cook you were."

"Anything for you, sweet lady." He leaned over and gave her a peck on the lips. "You're worth all the effort." He took another bite. "Mmm... dang! This is good, even for me!"

They continued their small talk through dinner. Pete kept adding small amounts of the chardonnay to their glasses. As the sipped, Brianna felt herself laughing more at Pete's corny jokes. He cleared the dishes from the table and suggested they have dessert on the couch in the living room. He brought over a small plate with ice cream sitting on top of a slice of cake, all of it drizzled with hot fudge. He had one spoon. "I thought we could share." He scooped up a little of each piece, and fed it to Brianna.

"Mmm... that's delicious," she purred. She licked her lips, then held them open, waiting for another bite. Pete obliged, teasing her with the spoon until she was reaching for the dessert herself.

"You have some chocolate sauce on your lips," he said. "Let me clean it up." He leaned in and ever so slightly licked the sauce from lips. "That was tasty."

"Yes, it was," she replied, breathless.

He leaned in closer so his lips were barely touching hers. "Would you like some more?"

"Yes, please." Before she finished the words, she felt Pete's lips on hers, gently, tentatively probing, seeking her permission to explore further. She gave her unspoken consent by returning the kiss, softly, then more urgently. When they pulled apart for air, Pete moved from her lips to her jaw, adding kisses down her neck. Brianna moaned her delight when Pete found her sweet spot at the base of her neck. His hand moved up her body and across her breast, rubbing, then stroking her nipple area. His lips continued their descent down the opening of her blouse towards her cleavage. Pete opened her blouse, his hand sliding first across her bra, then inside, tugging her breast out of its restraint.

The motion jarred Brianna and her breath caught. "Stop. Pete, stop."

"Mmm... c'mon, Bri."

"No, Pete. Stop." She grabbed his wrist and pulled it back. "Stop. We can't."

"What do you mean? What's wrong? If I'm going too fast, I can slow down. I've got protection."

"No, it's not that. We just can't do this. I made a vow to the Lord. I'm keeping it."

"Aw, not that this again." He let out a string of expletives and headed for the bathroom.

Brianna caught her breath. *Lord, forgive me. This was a mistake.* As she began straightening out her clothes, she heard a buzzing from the couch. She glanced over and saw Pete's phone. Curious, she picked it up and gasped. A woman named Angel had sexted him a half-naked picture of herself with the caption: "When you're ready for a real woman."

When Pete came back, he was much more together. "Bri, I'm sorry about that. I guess it was the wine. Things were going so well between us and I got a little frustrated."

"Then I guess I'm not the right woman for you. Your real Angel is waiting," she said, holding out his phone to him.

"What were you doing with my phone? Were you spying on me?"

She laughed. "I wasn't spying. Your phone told me everything I needed to know all on its own. Tell me the truth, Pete. Why did you come back into my life?"

"I told you, I love you."

"You don't love me, Pete. Not really. If you did, you wouldn't have brought wine. You wouldn't have pushed me into making out with you."

"Whoa, hold on. You make it sound like I was forcing you. I didn't force anything on you. You were clearly enjoying yourself as much as I was."

"I'm sorry. I didn't mean to make it sound like that. What I meant was, you wouldn't have put us in the position that we were in. It's as much my fault as yours, though. I knew better. I knew what I was doing. And you're right: I was enjoying myself. But whatever temporary pleasure I would have experienced with you would not have been worth breaking my promise to the Lord."

Pete advanced towards her and caressed her shoulders. "Bri, honey, God would understand. And he'd forgive us."

She pulled back. "And you've proven my point. I don't want to do something I know is wrong and have to ask forgiveness later. If you really loved me like you said you did, you'd understand."

Frustrated, he grabbed his jacket. "I'm not going to argue with you about this. You're all hung up trying to be this holy-holy good girl."

"And you're clearly looking for an easier route to getting what you want. You say you want an angel, but you're getting the devil in disguise."

"I'm outta here. Good night."

"Goodbye, Pete. Do me a favor? Stay gone."

CHAPTER TWENTY-TWO

"I blew it, Liz," Brianna lamented to her friend. It was the Friday after her disastrous dinner with Pete. She twirled a strand of hair between her fingers, a sure sign of anxiety. "I should have dropped Pete before he ever got a chance to worm his way back into my life. I let a good man slip away."

"Stop beating yourself up," Liz replied. "You were scared to jump in a relationship with Jake. You went for what was comfortable and familiar, and it blew up in your face. At least now you have your answer."

"Daddy was right. When I took myself out of the prayer and just asked God to reveal the truth, Pete's true colors came out. It was clear as glass. I can't believe I couldn't see it before."

"You didn't want to see it, *chica*."

"Yeah, I'm so aware."

"Have you tried calling Jake?"

"I have. He hasn't returned my calls. I don't think he wants anything to do with me."

"That's not true. Luis said they still prayed for you on their call. I think he misses you."

"If that were true, why hasn't he returned my calls?"

"To make you suffer?"

"Liz!"

"Well, you did blow him off at Bella's party. I'd make you suffer a bit too."

"I tried to apologize. I just couldn't do it over the phone." A thought occurred to her. "Wait, when did Luis last talk to Jake?"

"Um… Monday night, I think."

"What about since then?"

Liz paused. "I don't know. Maybe." She covered her phone and called out for her husband. "Luis, have you spoken to Jake since Monday?"

"Not since our prayer call," Luis responded.

"Isn't that strange?" Liz asked. "Do you think something happened to him?"

"Something happened to Jake?" Brianna exclaimed. "Put Luis on the phone!"

Liz replied, "I'm putting you on speaker."

"Who's on the phone?" Luis asked.

"It's Bri," Liz replied.

"Oh, hey Bri."

"What happened to Jake? What do you know?" Brianna asked.

"He's okay. Well, he's been laid up for the last couple of days."

"What? Why?"

"He's been sick. He got the flu and it's knocked him out," Luis said.

"Who gets the flu in May?" Liz asked. "And why didn't you say anything?"

"He sent me a text yesterday. He turned off his phone so he could rest. I offered to bring him something, but he insisted I stay home so I wouldn't get the baby sick."

"Luis, I need a favor," Brianna said.

***

Brianna bribed the doorman in Jake's building to let her upstairs, promising him a cup of the savory soup she was carrying to Jake. She took the elevator to the tenth floor, and headed to his apartment. *Lord, I don't know if he'll even let me in, but please help him to get better.*

She knocked at the door and waited. *This was a stupid idea. Maybe I should just leave the soup with a note.* Except she knew she had no paper or pen in her mini purse. Her stomach growled as she inhaled the aroma of the homemade soup that Luis had made.

The door opened, and a striking brunette, 6'2", lean but muscular, with a pixie haircut stood in the doorway. "Can I help you?"

"I'm... I'm Brianna. I'm a friend of Jake's."

The other woman smiled. "Oh hey! It's nice to finally meet you. I'm Ollie Taylor. Jake and I work together."

"Ollie?"

"Short for Olivia. Come on in." As Brianna passed by her, she sniffed. "What in heaven's name is that delicious smell?"

"It's homemade chicken soup."

"You made that?"

Brianna laughed. "Not even close. A friend of mine—of ours—made it for him. I just offered to bring it over." *Relax, girl. Stop sounding so possessive. He's not yours—yet.* "Can you show me to the kitchen?"

"Sure, but only if I can snag a bowl."

"Done." Ollie led the way to Jake's kitchen. It was surprisingly spacious for the apartment, with a double convection oven and a six-burner stove, double wall fridge, all stainless steel. Brianna loved how the seemingly masculine appliances were contrasted with warmer hues of green, red and brown.

"You seem surprised," Ollie said.

"I haven't been here before."

"I see." Ollie eyed her curiously. "You didn't know that your friend was a budding Iron Chef?"

Brianna shook her head. "No. We've only been out a couple of times. He mentioned he liked to cook, but I didn't expect a gourmet kitchen." She set the pot on the stove and set it on simmer. It was still warm, but she wanted to get a better read on Ollie. "How long have you known Jake?"

"What you really want to know is how well I know him. I've known him since the academy. Jake is like a brother to me. We went out once, but there was zero chemistry, thankfully."

"Why thankfully?"

"If we had been involved, it wouldn't have worked. We're too much alike and we'd wind up killing each other. It would have destroyed our friendship and working relationship. And I never would have met my wonderful husband." She pulled out her phone and scrolled through some photos. "Here's my hubby, Craig."

Brianna smiled. Jake had one arm slung around a handsome, dark-haired, blue-eyed white man and another around Ollie. Ollie flipped the photo and Jake was being "horsey" to an adorable set of toddlers. "Yours?"

"Yep. Matty is three and Celia is two."

"Wow. They're gorgeous." Brianna sized up the other woman's lean, toned frame. "You don't look like you've had two kids back to back."

"One of the true blessings of this job. I stayed active right up until delivery and I shed the pounds as quickly as I could. I couldn't do this job carrying an extra thirty or forty pounds."

They heard a shuffling sound and turned to see a weakened Jake leaning in the doorway. "Brianna? What are you doing here?"

"That's my cue," Ollie said. "I'm heading out." She went over and patted Jake on his shoulder. "I think you're in good hands. See you soon, brother."

"What about your soup?" Brianna called out.

"Next time," Ollie replied, grinning.

CHAPTER TWENTY-THREE

Brianna waited until she heard the front door close, then began busying herself in the kitchen looking for bowls and spoons for the soup.

"What are you doing here?" Jake asked again.

"I brought you some soup," she replied, not looking at him.

"Soup?"

"Yes. Luis said you had the flu, so I brought you some soup."

"I see." He sat down at the island in the kitchen. "It smells good. Did you make it?"

"I wish. Luis made it. He says it'll kill or cure what ails you. I can testify to that."

"What's in it?"

"Family recipe," she answered. "He said if he told me what's in it, he'd have to kill me."

"Bri?"

"Yes?"

"You haven't answered my question."

"What question?" she asked, feigning innocence.

"Why are you here?"

"I told you—soup."

"Brianna. Stop. Turn around and look at me."

She paused her movement, but she did not turn around. He said again, "Look at me."

She turned, slowly. It took every ounce of her will to look him in the face. She took a deep breath and blurted, "I brought you soup because you were sick. But it was just an excuse to see you. I've been calling and you didn't return my messages. I didn't think you wanted to see me again. But I wanted to see you, and I figured in your weakened condition, you'd at least let me give you soup."

He smiled crookedly. "Really. You wanted to see me again?"

"Yes."

"Why?"

She bit her lip and shifted her weight. "I was wrong."

"About?"

He's enjoying torturing me. Might as well get it over with. "The truth is, I was wrong to end things with you before they even got started good. The whole thing with Pete was a disaster."

"So, I was your plan B?"

"No! I mean," she sighed, "you were never plan B. With Pete, it was comfortable, it was familiar. We had history, and I felt like I owed it to myself to see if there was still something there."

"And was there?" He coughed. Brianna found a glass and went in his fridge and poured him some orange juice. He took a sip. "Thanks. Was there something there?"

"Yes, but it was nothing I wanted to be a part of. The reason we broke up in the first place was because I was serious about my relationship with Christ, which meant no more sex until we were married. He couldn't handle it, which is why he ghosted me the first time."

"Why did he come back?"

She shrugged. "I don't know. I thought he had a change of heart. He acted like he did. He said and did all the right things. But it wasn't real. He wasn't real. I couldn't see it. Or maybe I didn't want to see it."

"How did you figure it out?"

She smiled. "My dad helped me. I told him what I was struggling with. I told him about you."

Jake's grin grew broader. "Really? What did you tell him?"

"That's not the point. Anyway, I told him I was mixed up about the two of you and how I felt like God wasn't answering my prayers. Daddy said I shouldn't be praying for which one I should be with, but for discernment about you and Pete, that your true character would reveal itself." Remembering that night and how far they'd nearly gone, Brianna blushed and turned back to the stove. "Let's just say, my eyes were clearly opened. I kicked Pete out of my life for good. That chapter is closed once and for all." She ladled a bowl of the piping hot soup and added a small dinner roll to a small saucer, then placed them both in front of him. "Watch out, it's hot."

"Thanks." He gestured for her to sit. "Have dinner with me."

"Are you sure?"

"Beats eating alone. Besides, we haven't finished our conversation."

She nodded, then went and fixed a bowl for herself. She pulled out a bottle of hand sanitizer and set it between them. At his puzzled look, she took his hand and bowed her head, then blessed the food. When she was done, she sanitized her hands. "I have to be at work Monday morning. I'm all out of sick days."

Over the next hour, they ate and shared small talk. Jake was curious about Brianna's parents and their reaction to having two men in her life. Brianna learned more about Jake's work and his relationships with his fellow troopers, who were more family than co-workers. He also told her about his brother, Desmond. It was clear that there was a tight bond between them.

"Whew," he finally said. "This is probably the longest I've been up in days. I'm beat. But I'm not ready to go back to bed."

"Why don't we go to the living room and watch a movie?"

"What's on?"

"I'm game for anything but horror."

"Suits me fine." He started to stand but nearly tipped over. "Whoa."

Brianna jumped up to steady him. "Take it easy there, big fella." She wrapped her arm around his torso to steady him, acutely aware of chiseled frame being so close to her. Under different circumstances...

"I hope you weren't planning on taking advantage of me in my weakened condition."

"No... of course not."

"Darn," Jake whispered.

CHAPTER TWENTY-FOUR

Jake felt someone tapping his knee. "Jake? Why don't you go to bed?"

"Why don't you come with me," he muttered.

"Jake!"

He felt a slap on his knee. His eyes flew open as he saw a grinning Brianna standing over him. "Uh...," he stammered.

"That was some dream you were having, mister."

He groaned and dropped his head in his hands. "Did I say that out loud?"

She laughed. "You did. We'll blame it on the soup." She held out her hands. "Let me help you up. I don't want you tipping over with nothing to break your fall."

Nothing except you. "How long have I been out?"

"Not long, just a couple of hours."

"I haven't been very good company."

"Nonsense. You've had the flu. It's to be expected."

"What time is it?"

"Nearly midnight." She yawned. "I should be getting home."

"You should stay." At her dismayed expression, he said, "It's late. I don't want you driving home by yourself. And you're probably drowsy as well. Driving when you're sleepy is as bad as driving while intoxicated, and the results can be just as disastrous. Please, just crash here for the night."

She stifled another yawn. "You're probably right. Okay. I'll get you tucked in and I'll crash on the couch." She motioned for him to stand. He grasped her hands as she helped him pull up. He swayed in place for a moment, allowing his equilibrium to stabilize. Once again, she wrapped her arm around him and they began the slow walk towards his bedroom. He couldn't tell if it was the flu or just being so close to her that was making him weak in the knees. If nothing else, Jake knew he liked the way she felt being so close to him. Her torso and height easily melded with his, as if fitting two interlocking puzzle pieces together. He smiled at the thought: maybe Brianna was the missing piece in his life after all.

When they got to his room, he nearly collapsed in his bed. He sensed something was different, but he was too tired to think what it was. He just knew he was glad to be in his own bed and glad Brianna had agreed to stay the night.

CHAPTER TWENTY-FIVE

As sunlight peeked through the blinds of his bedroom, Jake slowly opened his eyes. For the first time in a week, he felt almost human. Whatever Luis had put in the soup, it seemed to have done the trick. He stretched, yawned, and sat up slowly, gauging his strength level. He rotated his neck, then paused. That fleeting thought he had before he fell asleep returned: the sheets on his bed were different. How did that happen? Normally, he changed his sheets every week, but after falling ill, he hadn't bothered since he'd been practically bedridden all week.

He stood, and for the first time, the room didn't seem to be spinning. He walked out and looked around the living room. He smiled when he saw Brianna still sleeping on the couch. She was covered in one of his grandmother's handmade quilts and had found one of his extra bed pillows. She looked peaceful—and incredibly beautiful. He wanted to rouse her with a kiss, but a quick sniff made him realize he'd be better off after a shower.

He was just about to turn in his bathroom, when he stole a glance at his small laundry room. Brianna had washed and folded his previous bed linens, plus a basket full of towels. "God, thank you for this amazing woman you've sent my way," he whispered.

He spent the next fifteen minutes attending to his personal hygiene. After slipping on jogging suit, he headed for the kitchen and smiled again. Everything in the room was pristine. He checked the dishwasher and found it empty. The pot that Brianna brought the soup in was washed and dried and sat neatly on the counter out of the way. Humming a worship song to himself, he began brewing a pot of coffee. Then he decided to make breakfast. Still unsure if he'd be able to hold everything down, he settled on a pot of grits, scrambled eggs and toast. He made a small platter of bacon and sausage for Brianna as well.

"Mmm... something smells good," Brianna said, standing in the doorway. "Luis' soup must have done its magic."

"I'll say it did." He poured a cup of coffee and offered it to her. "I made breakfast for us."

"I can't wait. Let me wash my face and I'll be ready." She headed down the hallway, already seemingly comfortable in his apartment. *Yes, Lord. She's the real deal. I hope she feels the same way.*

A few minutes later, she took a seat at the counter where Jake had set the food and the flatware. He couldn't help but notice she was without a stitch of makeup, yet she fairly glowed. She had pulled her bedhead hair into a semblance of a ponytail, yet it still looked fresh and styled.

"Um, Jake?"

"Yes?"

"You wanna bless the food?"

He sheepishly looked down at the counter. She caught him staring and lost in his thoughts again. He hoped she attributed it to his recovery from the flu. He quickly blessed the food, and they began to eat.

Every once in a while, Brianna would eat a forkful of grits. She would let out a little moan that both delighted and enticed Jake. All he could think about was kissing her and hearing her moan like that for him. *Whoa, buddy. Slow it down. Neither of us is ready to go there yet. Okay, maybe I am. But she's not. I think.* "Everything okay over there?"

"What? Oh yes. Oh, my goodness, Jake, these grits! Baby bye! My daddy would kill for some of these grits. Mama always made them, but they were gritty, hard. These are so smooth. What's your secret?"

"Slow cooking and plenty of butter. I'm glad you like them."

"When my parents come by this summer, you'll have to cook some for them."

Hang on. Did she just say what I think she did? "When are your folks coming up?"

"Around the fourth of July. Liz and Luis host this amazing family picnic and Luis and Ronaldo put up an unbelievable firework show. The whole neighborhood comes out to see it. I know they'll be expecting us to come."

Us? He paused his eating, deciding he needed to hear from her clearly what he was hearing in his mind and his heart. "Bri, we need to finish our conversation from last night."

She nodded and took a sip of her coffee. "I know. I just wanted to do it on a full stomach."

"Do you want to finish your food?"

"Not yet. I think if I polish this off, I'll be ready for a nap."

"I understand. But before you talk, I have a question."

"Shoot."

"When did you wash the linens? And why?"

"That's two questions, but I'll answer them both. Once you got comfortable in the chair, you passed out cold. I was watching the movie, but I had to use the bathroom. I passed by your room, and it smelled, well, funky. Like sick, funky. I decided to wash everything. I figured you'd rest better on fresh linens. Did I do something wrong?"

"No. I've just…other than my mother, I've never had a woman do my laundry before."

"Really? None of your exes did that?"

He shook his head. "Nope. That's partially why they're exes. They weren't exactly the domestic types."

"And I am?" she replied, grinning.

"Well, the sheets do smell April fresh." He ducked as she tossed a piece of toast at him.

CHAPTER TWENTY-SIX

Brianna ate another forkful of grits. They were absolutely delicious, but the truth was, she was stalling. She knew Jake wouldn't wait much longer. She took a deep breath. "Thanks for breakfast," she said.

"Anytime," he replied. He took one of her hands in his. "Are you ready to talk?"

She nodded. "As ready as I'll ever be, I guess." She glanced away from him. If she told him everything, she was sure he would ask her to leave. Yet, she knew if she wasn't honest with him, he would never trust her and that would destroy them. "I need to tell you what happened between Pete and me. I told you were involved previously. When he came back into my life, I honestly thought we could start over again. After I talked with my dad, I prayed in earnest. I really wanted God to show me the truth.

"Pete came over and cooked me dinner. It was wonderful. I talked and he listened, something he hadn't been very good at in the past. But one drink led to another, and one kiss led to…" She tried not to gasp as he pulled his hand away from hers. She looked him full in the face. His features had hardened and his countenance darkened. *Show me his real character, Lord.* "One kiss led to another and before I knew it, we were heading down a familiar path. But, as the old folks say, 'something got a-hold of me.' I put a stop to things before they got out of hand."

"Did he… did he…"

"No! When I said stop, he stopped. Pete may be a lot of things, but he's not that kind of man. He wasn't happy, and he tried to convince me that we were good, but then God showed up. Pete's phone rang and while he was in the bathroom, I picked it up and saw his booty call on full blast. I kicked him out, blocked his number and thanked God that he had stopped me from making the biggest mistake of my life."

Jake's features softened. "Is that the end of it?"

"It is as far as I'm concerned. I told security at the school if he showed up, they were to escort him out. I never want to see him again." She sniffed as a tear escaped. "I tried to call you and tell you that, but you didn't respond. I thought for sure I had lost you forever."

Jake reached up and wiped the tear. "I didn't realize you had called. I changed my phone and not all of my numbers transferred. Then I got the flu and I've been waylaid ever since." He took her hand again. "Since I didn't get the message, why don't you tell me what you would have said?"

"I—um," she laughed. "This is silly."

"Tell me."

"Okay, fine." She changed the pitch of her voice so it was very girly. "Hi Jake, I miss you, call me."

"Really?"

"No." She dropped the smile, then picked up his other hand in hers. "Hi Jake. This is Brianna. First, let me say how sorry I am. I hurt you and that's the last thing I ever wanted to do. I was wrong to try and play you against my ex. I should have been honest with you from the beginning. I'm done with him, and I'm done playing games. I know you're a good man and I'd like another shot. I hope you'll forgive me and—" Her next words were cut off by Jake's mouth covering hers in a breathtaking kiss.

When he released her, she whispered, "Does this mean you've forgiven me?"

"There's nothing to forgive," he replied. "You had me at hi."

CHAPTER TWENTY-SEVEN

Brianna was grateful that her career in education afforded her time off in the summer. As happy as she was to see her students each fall, she was equally happy when the school year ended, satisfied that most, if not all of her students were ready to move on to the next grade. She also badly needed time to rest and recharge her batteries and begin to plan for the next school year.

This year, she was especially grateful that she did not have to teach summer school, but instead could use her time to spend in her growing relationship with Jake. When his schedule changed, she was easily able to adapt from a morning brunch to a late-night dinner and movie. It didn't matter what they did, as long as they did it together. The rush of love they felt for each other was unlike anything either of them had experienced.

It was Jake who first expressed how he felt on a date soon after his recovery from the flu. Deciding to take it easy on his first day out after being cooped up for a week, they decided to take a walk in the park near his apartment. Brianna's heart stopped when they encountered a crying toddler walking by herself. Brianna knelt down and spoke to the little girl. "Hi, sweetie. Are you lost?"

"Mommy sick," the girl managed to say through her tears.

"Okay, it's gonna be okay. What's your name, sweetie?"

"Ri-rey."

"Riley?" The girl nodded. "Where's your mommy?"

"Mommy sick."

"I know. Can you tell me where she is so we can help her?" The little girl turned and pointed towards the playground.

Jake went into rescue mode. "Stay here. I don't know what I'll find." He jogged off in the direction Riley had pointed.

"I want Mommy!" Riley screamed.

Brianna pulled the little girl close. "I know Riley, I know. Listen, my friend is a police officer. He's gonna go check on your mom and get her some help, okay?"

"Okay," Riley sniffed.

"In the meantime, I need you to try and be a big girl for me, okay? I'm gonna stay with you until my friend comes back and then we'll find out what's happening with your mommy, okay?" She reached into her purse and pulled out a small pack of tissues and began wiping the girl's tear-stained face. "Can you tell me what happened to your mommy?"

Riley nodded. "Mommy fell down and then she fell asleep."

"Has she done it before?"

She nodded. "Daddy takes care of her."

"Okay. Do you know your daddy's name or phone number?" The little girl shook her head. "Do you know where your daddy is right now?"

"Work," Riley replied. "I want my daddy," she sniffled.

Brianna pulled the girl into a hug and rubbed her blonde curls. "Shhh...," she cooed. "It's gonna be okay. We're gonna find your daddy and your make sure your mommy is okay."

She was still holding Riley when Jake jogged back. "I found her."

"Is she..." Brianna whispered.

Jake shook his head. "She's alive. It looks like she had a grand mal seizure. She was wearing a Medic Alert bracelet. I called it in and called for an ambulance. They should be here in a few minutes."

"Did you find any ID or a cell phone? Riley says this has happened before, but her dad usually takes care of her."

He nodded. "I'll check at the scene." He touched the little girl on her shoulder and as she turned around, Jake had a huge grin on his face. "Hi Riley. I'm Jake. I'm a police officer." He pulled out his badge and showed it to her.

"Mommy sick," Riley repeated.

"I know, but I just saw her and she's going to be okay. I called an ambulance, and they're coming so they can take her to the hospital to see a doctor." The wail of the siren distracted Jake. He stood as the paramedics rushed over. "You two stay here. We're gonna go take care of your mom." Jake led the paramedics to the playground.

***

Riley insisted on being with her mother, so she and Brianna rode in the ambulance. The entire ride, Brianna talked to Riley, comforting the little girl as the paramedic did her job. Brianna had to calm the girl again once they rushed her mother into an exam room and Riley began to cry.

An hour later, Brianna was still sitting in the waiting area. Riley had fallen asleep, and she had her head resting in Brianna's lap. The entire time, she stroked the little girl's head, alternately humming or praying as she watched over her sleeping charge.

Jake watched in awe. Brianna never took her eyes off the little girl. He had asked if she wanted something to eat or drink, and she replied with a shake of her head. She was so focused on the child's comfort, she had no awareness of anything else. Even after Riley's father rushed into the emergency room frantically searching for his wife, Brianna's focus never wavered. Jake greeted the harried man and together they found a nurse who showed the man where his wife was being treated.

Jake looked up and then tapped Brianna's leg. "Her father is here," he said.

Only then did Brianna look up into the worried, but grateful blue eyes of Riley's father. "She's okay," she said. She shook the girl gently, "Riley? Honey, wake up. Your daddy's here." She continued gently shaking her, rousing her from her exhausted slumber. "Wake up, Riley. Daddy's here."

The little girl stretched then fluttered open a pair of matching blue eyes. "Hi Daddy," she whispered, stretching out her arms.

The man quickly scooped her up in his arms and gave her a reassuring hug. "Hi, Lovebug. I'm here."

"Mommy's sick," Riley said.

"Yeah, Mommy was sick. But she's much better now," her father said.

"I wanna see Mommy."

"How about we both go see her in a few minutes?" her father asked.

"Yay!" Riley cheered. She snuggled up in her father's chest and soon drifted back to sleep.

The man sighed. "I don't know how to thank you for what you did for Riley and my wife. Diane has epilepsy, but it's controlled by medication. Sometimes, she has seizures at home, but it's usually not that bad. This is the first time it's happened while she was out with our daughter. She usually takes Riley out to play in the afternoon, but only for a half hour or so. I was in a meeting and I didn't have a chance to check in. When I called the house and she didn't answer, I tried her cell. But when she didn't pick up, I wasn't worried at first. But when she didn't call me back, I got worried. Thankfully, the doctor said she's going to be just fine."

"You have a really beautiful daughter," Brianna said.

"I thank God that it was the two of you that found her. When I think of what could have happened to Riley if the wrong person found her," he blinked back tears. "I'm just grateful you both for taking care of my family."

"God brought us there at the right time and the right place," Jake said.

"Amen," Brianna agreed. "Do you mind if we pray for you and your family, uh…"

"Austin. Austin Sheridan. And no, I don't mind."

Quietly, Brianna laid her hand on Austin's shoulder and joined Jake's hand and led them all in prayer, thanking God for Diane's recovery, for Riley's safety and Austin's peace of mind. At the end of the prayer, Riley murmured, "'men," causing the adults to laugh.

Austin stood. "I should be getting back to Diane. Again, thank you both so much for helping my family and staying with Riley. If there's anything I can ever do for you…"

"We were happy to be of service," Brianna said. "Take care of your family." She leaned in and gave the toddler a peck on the cheek. "Bye Riley."

"Brianna," Riley whined, reaching over to hug her rescuer. "I love you."

"I love you, too, sweet girl."

As she and Jake walked out, his arm wrapped around her shoulder, he leaned in, pulled her close, and whispered, "I love you, Brianna."

She stopped in her tracks, mouth agape. "What did you just say?"

Jake paused, unsure if she would be receptive. "I said, I love you. I've been wanting to tell you that for the longest time. I just wasn't sure how you felt. But after watching you today, how you cared for Riley like she was your own child, how you prayed for that family without hesitation, I knew I couldn't go another day without telling you how I feel. I hope—I pray you feel the same, or you're getting there."

For a response, Brianna stepped up and grabbed his face in her hands and kissed him. After a minute, she stepped back, then wiped a stray tear and smiled. "I love you too, Jake. I was scared to say anything, especially after my mistake with Pete. I wanted to tell you that morning after I spent the night at your place, but I thought it would have been too soon, or maybe you thought I was just on a rebound. I do love you, Jake Lewis, more than I ever thought I could love anyone."

"Oh baby," he said, pulling her into another kiss. When he pulled back, he said, "I can't wait to meet your parents."

CHAPTER TWENTY-EIGHT

The Fourth of July weekend was hot and muggy in Chicago, which was typical. Brianna didn't mind the heat, but she absolutely despised the humidity, which always made her feel like she needed a shower. As much as she loved the idea of the party Luis and Liz had planned, she secretly hoped it would rain so they could hang out inside the Trujillo's air-conditioned house.

Truth be told, the real reason she had been sweating was the fact that her parents were in town and they were going to meet Jake for the first time. Ernest and Lucille Norwood had heard many good things from their daughter about the man she had fallen in love with, but had withheld their blessing until they had a face-to-face meeting.

The doorbell rang and Brianna nearly jumped out of her skin. *Settle down girl; settle down.* She took in a deep breath and released it, then headed for the door. Jake stood there looking as dapper as ever in a short sleeve polo shirt and a pair of khaki carpenter slacks. He greeted her with a kiss and she let him in. "You ready to go?"

"Yeah, just let me get the deviled eggs out the fridge."

He took her hands in his. "You okay? Your hands are shaking."

"I'm fine. I'm just really nervous about you meeting my parents."

"You said they would like me."

"I said, I'm pretty sure they'll like you. My track record hasn't been the best when it comes to men I've been involved with. They are going to be pretty rough on you."

"I can handle it, Bri. I just want them to know how crazy I am about their daughter and that I'd never do anything to hurt her."

She smiled. "Okay. We got this. Let's get the rest of the food."

***

The Trujillo house was bustling with activity by the time Jake and Brianna arrived. Both mothers were in the kitchen cooking up a storm and barking orders at anyone that crossed their paths. Luis was outside manning the barbeque grill. Ronaldo was filling up the coolers with ice and beverages.

"*Hola,* Mama," Brianna called out cheerfully. "Where's Liz?"

"She's putting Bella down for a nap," Liz's mother, Julia, replied. "Put those eggs in the fridge," she said.

"Is there anything you need me to do?"

"*Sí,*" Luis' mother, Alma, replied. "You can stir the beans."

"What about me?" Jake asked.

"You go out with the boys and help them. Go, get out of our kitchen," Luis' mother, Alma, said. She began muttering something in Spanish to Julia, Liz's mother, which had them both dissolving into laughter.

"I don't know what they said," Jake whispered to Brianna, "but something tells me I'd be better off with Luis."

"Good call," she replied, giving him a peck on the lips. As she watched him walk out to the patio, Julia called out, "Beans, *mija*, beans!"

After a few minutes of stirring, the mothers put Brianna to work shucking corn on the cob. Liz entered the kitchen and laughed. "They got you too, huh?"

"I offered," Brianna. "My goddaughter finally asleep?"

"Not yet. She's hearing all the fuss and music and she won't go down. I gave up and put her in her playpen. She'll either go down on her own, or be Miss Crankypants all afternoon." She pulled up a chair and grabbed an ear of corn. Lowering her voice, she said, "Today's the big day, huh? You nervous?"

Brianna nodded. "Jake's a wonderful guy, but you know how my dad is. And all mom wants is a little Bella of her own."

"Jake can handle Ernie and Mama 'Cille. He got by Luis, and you know he's like the older brother you never had."

"I guess."

"What's really going on? I mean besides the whole meet the parents thing."

Brianna shrugged. "Jake told me he has to work tonight. I was hoping he'd be off the entire weekend."

"Awww, it's so cute when you're in love and you never want to be apart," Liz teased.

Brianna threw a corn husk at her. "It's not that, silly. It's just my parents are only here for the weekend and I wanted the four of us to spend as much time together as we could. Mom's going to have her knee replacement surgery in a couple of weeks and she won't be able to travel for a while. I'm going to stay with them for a week or so after to help around the house. By the time I get back, we'll be in full prep mode for school. With his schedule, sometimes it's hard to get some quality time together."

"You'll have plenty of time together, trust me," Liz said.

Before she could ask what her friend meant, she spotted her parents coming through the kitchen. "Daddy," Brianna cried. She dropped the ear of corn and rushed over to give her father a hug.

Ernest was carrying a wiggling Bella in his arms. "This little angel was trapped in a cage, but I rescued her, didn't I sweet girl," he declared, giving her a raspberry on her cheek, which caused her to burst in a fit of giggles.

Lucille, Ernest's wife, followed behind, leaning on her cane. "I'm sorry, Liz. She was almost down and the minute he came through the door, she jumped up and he couldn't resist." She gave her daughter a giant squeeze and a kiss on the cheek.

"It's okay, Mama 'Cille," Liz replied. "I suspect she wasn't actually going to sleep anyway." She hopped up and hugged the older couple, and tried to wrestle her daughter away, but she wouldn't let go of Ernest.

"What can I tell you? The ladies love me," Ernest boasted. "Ain't that right, Alma and Julia?"

"Ha!" Julia declared. "You know you only got eyes for 'Cille." She wiped her hands on her apron then scooted round Ernest to give her old friend a hug. "Now you come on in and take a seat. Rest that knee, 'Cille." She escorted the other woman to a chair, even as Lucille fussed.

"I'm fine, Julia. Alma, how are you?"

"I'm blessed," Luis' mom replied, "*gloria a Dios*. You want something to drink?"

"I could go for something cold," Ernest replied.

"Same," Lucille replied.

"I'll get it," Brianna answered. She shot Liz a quick look then darted out the patio door. A few minutes later, she returned with two bottles of water in her hands, and Jake right behind her. "Mom, Dad, this is Jake Lewis. Jake, these are my parents, Ernest and Lucille Norwood." Brianna handed her parents the waters she had brought in.

"It's nice to finally meet you, Mr. Norwood, Mrs. Norwood," Jake said, shaking their hands. "Brianna has told me a lot about you."

"Yes, and we've heard a lot about you, too," Lucille replied, smiling. "Please sit down."

"Yes ma'am."

"No, no, it's not ma'am. Everyone calls me Mama 'Cille."

"And I'm Ernie," her father said. "Brianna tells me you're a state trooper."

"Yes sir, Ernie. I am. I've been there almost eleven years."

"What about your family?" Lucille asked.

Jake shrugged. "It's just my older brother, Desmond, and me. Our parents were killed in a car accident when I was sixteen."

"I'm so sorry," Lucille said.

"Thank you. I know I'll see them again."

Ernest asked, "What were they like?"

Jake chuckled. "My folks were great. Dad worked at the Ford plant, but he was also a Sunday School teacher. Mom worked as a school secretary. They always were around for every school performance, PTA meeting or parent/teacher conference. They believed in education and discipline. If we weren't doing chores or in some type of activity for school or church, they expected us to have our heads in a book. I didn't mind, but Des hated it. He signed up for every activity he could. He played football, basketball, and track. He was good, too. He got a full ride to college. But after our parents died, he switched gears. He came home and took a job to look out for me. Once I graduated from high school, Des enrolled in the Marines and never looked back. He's a sergeant stationed at Kaneohe Bay in Honolulu. He loves it there. He's always trying to convince me to move."

"But you opted to stay here," Lucille said.

"Yes ma'am. Chicago is my home. There's no place like it in the world. Besides, if I'd have left," he looked up at Brianna, "I'd have missed the biggest blessing of my life."

"Oh, that's wonderful, Jake," Lucille said.

Jake turned to Ernest. "Sir…"

"Call me Ernie."

"Yes, sir—Ernie. I was wondering if I could have a word with you in private?"

"Yes, of course." He stood. "Why don't we head into the living room?" He glanced down at Bella, who had finally drifted to sleep. "I'll put her down and we can talk."

As the two men exited, Brianna cast a puzzled glance towards her mother. "What's that all about?"

Lucille shrugged, then smiled. "Man talk."

CHAPTER TWENTY-NINE

An hour later, the party was in full swing. Luis had programmed his iPod with an eclectic mix of music featuring Spanish dance music, jazz, gospel and old school R&B. Several of the Trujillo's neighbors had stopped by with their families along with some of Brianna and Liz's colleagues from school and Luis' company. They all took turns dancing and eating the sumptuous meal that everyone had prepared. Jake, Luis, Ernest, and Ronaldo were having a spirited game of dominos. Bella's nap was short-lived and she was enjoying time playing on Lucille's lap and entertaining her grandmothers. Brianna and Liz emerged from the house carrying trays filled with homemade ice cream and gelato. They distributed them to the guests, getting kisses and high fives along the way. The joy of the moment was short-lived when a familiar voice boomed through the backyard.

"Heeeyyy fam! What's good!" Pete called out.

"Oh, my God," Brianna said.

"What is he doing here?" Liz whispered.

"I don't know," she answered. She passed her tray to her friend and rushed over. "What are you doing here, Pete?"

"Hey baby! It's good to see you!" He leaned over to kiss her, but she pulled back.

"What are you doing?" Brianna sniffed. "You've been drinking."

"You know, just trying to get the party started." He moved out of her grip and headed to where the men had halted their game and were now standing. Luis was the first to move. "Pete," he said, "dude, you really shouldn't be here. Let me get you a ride."

"Aw come on, man. We're friends, right?" He extended his hand towards Ernest. "Hey Pops. Good to see you man. How you been?"

Ernest frowned, but did not shake the man's hand. "Peter."

"Aw, so it's like that, huh. That's cool." He turned, then laughed. "Well, well, well, if ain't Barney Fife. I thought for sure you'd have skipped on back to Mayberry with Gomer and Goober."

"Pete, why don't we go inside and let me get you a cup of coffee," Jake said.

"It's too hot for coffee. Besides, I just came to see my girl and celebrate the holidays like a good American. Viva las Americas!" Pete yelled.

"Let me get this *pedazo de mierda* out of your house," Ronaldo growled. Luis held his brother back.

"Say, look, Bri-honey. Let's you and me get out of here and spend some quality time together," Pete said. "Let's—let's stay together," he began singing.

Brianna rushed over. "Yes, Pete, let's go and get you sobered up." She tried to pull him away, but he wouldn't move.

"Baby, I'm doing just fine," he said, words slurring. "If you want my body, and you think I'm sexy," he crooned.

"Pete! That's enough."

He grabbed her around her waist and pulled her in close. Lowering his voice, he said, "Now that's not what you said the last time I came over." He began grinding against her. "I was lickin' and suckin', and you were moaning—"

Ernest grabbed Pete by the shoulder and yanked him back. "You take your hands off my daughter!"

Pete turned around. "Get your hands off me, old man! I will knock you clean out!"

He reached back to take a swing, but Jake lunged forward and grabbed Pete's fist and twisted his arm behind his back. Grabbing Pete by the scruff of his neck, Jake whispered, "You already made a fool of yourself. It's time for you to go."

"Let go of me!"

"Let me make this perfectly clear. You are drunk and you are trespassing. I am going to walk you out of here and put you in a car and send you on your way. And you will leave without causing another problem, because if you don't, I will have you arrested for drunk and disorderly, trespass, and assault. Luis, call this dude an Uber."

"No problem. I'm on it," Luis replied.

"You lose that badge and I'd kick your ass," Pete growled.

Jake yanked Pete's neck again. "You come near Brianna, her parents, or her friends again, and you won't have to worry about my badge. But you will have to worry about me. Let's go."

CHAPTER THIRTY

Brianna sat on the ottoman in Bella's room wiping away tears. It was bad enough that Pete showed up drunk, embarrassing her in front of her parents and friends, but he had to throw up their recent dalliance in front of Jake. They had finally gotten on the same page in their relationship. A reminder of how close she had come to derailing it was the last thing she wanted to do. She looked up at a knock on the door. "Come in," she croaked.

Lucille came in followed by Liz, Julia and Alma. "You doing okay, sweetheart?" Lucille asked as she took a seat next to her daughter.

"Oh Mom, I can't believe he would stoop so low. Is he gone?"

Liz nodded "Luis was waiting on the Uber and trying to keep Jake and Ronaldo from kicking his butt."

Brianna turned to the other women. "I'm sorry about all this. You all worked so hard for this afternoon, and I ruined it."

"Oh hush, *mija*," Julia said. "You did nothing wrong. Except getting involved with that *bastardo*."

"Ma!" Liz exclaimed.

"What? 'Cille knows what I mean."

Lucille chuckled. "You only said what I was thinking."

"Mom!" Brianna cried.

"*Él probablemente tiene una pequeña polla,*" Alma said, sending Julia into a fit of giggles and causing Liz to blush.

"What did she say?" Brianna asked.

Liz rolled her eyes and translated for her friends. Brianna's eyes grew wide and Lucille let out a belly laugh. All the women laughed until tears were flowing from their eyes.

"Listen, *mija*," Julia said, after she managed to calm herself down. "Liz kissed more than her fair share of frogs before she landed her prince."

"Ha! Luis is no prince," Alma said. "But he is a good man and we are blessed that they found each other. Your Jake is a good man, too. Pete is your past. Cook that frog up and serve him on a platter."

Liz shook her head at her mother-in-law. "Mama's right, girl. Jake already knows what happened between you and Pete. That hasn't stopped him from being with you. I've seen the two of you together. What you have is real. Nothing that jerk can do is going to break you up. Plus, he got Luis and Ernie's seal of approval."

Brianna turned to her mother. "Mom, what do you think?"

Lucille smiled. "I think it takes a year to plan a wedding."

"Mom!" The women dissolved into laughter again. A knock on the door revealed Jake standing there.

"What's so funny?" he asked.

"It's girl talk," Lucille responded. "C'mon ladies. Let's leave these two alone to talk." The four women stood and giggled as they passed by Jake on the way out.

He sat down next to her. "You okay?"

She shrugged. "I'm sorry about today. Is he gone?"

Jake nodded. "The Uber came a little while ago. Luis paid the Uber driver extra to make sure Pete got in safely."

"I didn't invite him, Jake. I swear. I haven't talked to him since that night I kicked him out of the house."

"Whoa, Bri, slow down. I know you didn't invite him. You told me that you always spend the holiday with Luis and Liz. It didn't take much for Pete to figure it out."

"Why did he have to show up here, today of all days?"

"He was drunk. Maybe he thought if he humiliated you in front of your friends, I'd split. Having your parents here was just a bonus. If he'd been in his right mind, he'd never had tried it, especially not in front of your dad. I mean, he's six-four and two-fifty, all muscle. If he'd half a mind to, your dad could have put Pete in the ground without breaking a sweat. I jumped in to save your dad from doing time." He grinned then hunched her until she laughed. "C'mon. Let's get back to the party. I've got a couple of hours before I have to head to work."

"You're doing the DUI checkpoints again?"

"Yes. It's not difficult. Most people we pull over are sober. Those that have been drinking usually are fairly cooperative, even if they're being arrested. I'm hoping for a slow night, though history has shown holidays are anything but slow. And I've already had more than my share of fireworks." He laughed.

They stood and headed for the door. "Are you going to tell me what you ladies were talking about?"

She winked and said, "Girl talk."

CHAPTER THIRTY-ONE

Liz and Brianna were finishing up the dishes, enjoying a good laugh. Alma and Julia were having a cup of tea as Lucille rocked Bella to sleep. Luis and Ernest were watching a baseball game on TV. At the commercial break, the news anchor came on. "Breaking news: massive accident on the tollway. At least seven vehicles were involved and we're being told of at least two fatalities, including a state trooper. We'll have more details including a live report in our newscast."

"Daddy?" Brianna said. "What did they say? A trooper was killed? What happened?"

"I don't know, baby girl. Something about an accident on the tollway."

"Which one?"

"They didn't say," Luis replied. He grabbed his iPad. "Maybe I can find out something online."

"There's no reason to think the worst," Liz said.

"Maybe. You're right. I'll call Jake just to make sure he's okay." She began spinning around. "Where's my phone? Where's my phone?"

"It's here, *mija*," Julia said, holding it up. "You were charging it."

Brianna took the phone in her shaking hand. She clicked on Jake's number and waited. It went into voicemail. She called again with the same result. "He's not picking up. He always answers when I call or sends me a text."

"With everything that's going on, he could be really busy," Liz said. "Don't go there."

"But what if…"

"There's no point into going into what ifs," Lucille said, coming over to hug her daughter. "Jake told you this would be a busy night. He could be in the middle of a traffic stop. He could be assisting in an arrest. He could be doing any number of things where he can't call you right back. The best thing you can do is to pray for him until we know something for sure."

Luis said, "I'm not having much luck. Details are sketchy. We're going to have to wait until the news comes on."

"Oh God," Brianna moaned.

"Do you know where he was posted?" Luis asked.

"I'm not… I'm not sure. Wait." She checked the messages on her phone. "No, he doesn't say. I think he was covering for another trooper who called in." As she scrolled through her text messages, an idea hit her. "Ollie!"

"Who's Ollie?" Liz said.

"She's Jake's best friend on the force." She frantically began typing a message to her: U okay? Do you know if Jake's okay? He doesn't answer. "If anybody knows anything about Jake, she would."

"Let's just pray she wasn't involved in the accident," Alma said.

"Amen," Julia replied.

Father, let them both be okay, Brianna prayed silently. *I pray you'll be with the family of the officer who was killed.* Her phone pinged with a response from Ollie: *I'm fine. He's okay, but he was hurt. We're at Northwestern.* Brianna sighed as she brushed away tears. "Jake's okay, but he's been hurt. Ollie doesn't say how bad."

"Let's go," Luis said. "You're in no shape to drive, Bri."

"I'm coming with," Liz replied. "Mama?"

"We'll take care of Bella," Julia replied.

"I'll drive your mother to your house, sweetheart," Ernest said. "We'll wait to hear from you."

"What are you waiting for?" Lucille asked. "Go. Go!"

CHAPTER THIRTY-TWO

Traffic was relatively heavy for the holiday night. Still, Luis managed to shave ten minutes off the normal thirty-minute drive it would have taken to get to Northwestern Memorial Hospital. No one spoke, but Luis kept the radio tuned into the local news station. The brief mention of the accident on the highway came and went every few minutes, but there was little the newscaster shared that they didn't already know.

By the time Luis pulled up to the Emergency Department entrance, Brianna felt like she was going to throw up. This was literally her worst nightmare coming true. At the same time, she wasn't afraid of Jake's injuries. It was the thought of not being able to share her life with him that made her sick. She knew she was in love with him. Unqualified, without hesitation, without reservation. The only question that remained was whether she could live with the dangers his job entailed. Tonight was a prime example. She didn't know what had transpired in the accident, but

Jake had been injured. She wasn't even sure how serious his injuries were. But another trooper had lost his life. It could have just as easily been Jake.

Suddenly, her father's words came back to her: *If you live your life in fear of the unknown, you will always live in fear.* Brianna knew she had a choice to make: let Jake go and find someone who would be "safer," or accept that Jake was in God's hands, no matter how he chose to live his life.

Luis pulled up to the entrance of the emergency department, dropping off Brianna and Liz while he went to park. They found the admissions desk and Brianna asked the clerk, "Where can I find trooper Jake Lewis?"

"Are you a relative?" the woman asked.

"No, I'm a friend. I'm his girlfriend," Brianna replied.

"I'm sorry, miss. I can't let you go back unless you're a relative. Hospital rules," she said.

"Well, can you at least tell me how he is?"

"I'm sorry, no."

Brianna huffed in frustration. "Please, I just need to know if he's okay."

"I'm sorry."

Brianna slammed her hand on the counter, but Liz pulled her away before she could explode at the woman. "She's just doing her job, Bri."

"I know," Brianna replied. She rolled her eyes, then spun around. "Ollie!" She sprinted over and embraced the woman she had come to know as a good friend to both her and Jake. "Are you okay?"

"I'm fine," Ollie replied. "How are you holding up? Have you seen Jake yet?"

"Not yet," Brianna replied. "I can't get past Nurse Ratchet."

"That's not nice," Liz said. "She just doing her job."

Ollie glanced over at Liz and frowned. "And you are?"

"Sorry," Brianna said. "Olivia Taylor, this is my best friend, Elizabeth Trujillo. Liz, this is Ollie."

"It's nice to meet you," Liz said. "I'm glad you're okay."

"Thanks. It's nice to meet you, too," Ollie replied.

At that moment, Luis walked up to the women. Liz made the introductions. "Have you seen him yet?" he asked.

"Not yet," Brianna replied. "I can't get past the drill sergeant at the desk."

"I think I can help with that," Ollie said. She walked over to a tall, slender, dark-haired man in a lab coat. When she reached up and kissed him, Liz gasped, but Brianna laughed. As Ollie and the man walked over, Brianna broke out in a big grin.

"Craig! I didn't know you were working tonight," Brianna said.

"I was on my way out when I heard about the accident," he replied. "When I heard they were headed here, I stuck around."

Brianna caught Liz and Luis' puzzled expressions. "This is Craig Taylor, Ollie's husband. He's a radiologist here at the hospital." She continued the introductions, then asked, "Craig, can you take me back to see Jake? The nurse won't let me back because I'm not family."

"I think I can help. Come with me," Craig replied.

CHAPTER THIRTY-THREE

Craig guided Brianna through the doors of the emergency entrance. The clerk at the desk gave her a sideways glance, but said nothing as they passed. He checked in with the desk and the charge nurse directed them to Jake's bay. Brianna paused at the entrance and stared. Jake was resting, his eyes closed, an oxygen mask over his face. Suddenly, she had a flashback: she was the one laying in the hospital bed with a mask over her face. Jake was standing over her after her accident. She couldn't bear to look at him then because she was still reeling from Ron's death. Now, their roles were reversed, and she couldn't take her eyes off of him.

She gave him a once over. The monitors above him showed that everything in his body was operating at normal. The only thing she could see amiss was his hands, which were wrapped in gauze and bandages. "What happened?" she asked Craig.

"I'm not sure," he said. "But from what I can tell, he's likely going to be discharged tomorrow, as long as his vitals remain normal."

"Can I go in?"

"Sure. I'm going to wait outside with Ollie."

As he left, she looked around and found a stool and pulled it up next to his bed. She closed her eyes and breathed a sigh of relief. "Thank you, Father, for sparing Jake's life. Thank you for protecting Ollie. I pray for the family of the fallen officer, that you will comfort and keep them tonight and in the days to come."

"Amen," Jake whispered hoarsely.

Brianna opened her eyes to see the love of her life grinning at her under his mask. She leaned over and kissed him on his forehead. "Hey love."

He shook his head. "Nope. That won't do." He gingerly pulled at his oxygen mask, wincing as his fingers bent to pull it off his face. She pulled it aside and gave him a kiss on the lips, mindful of the fact they were in a public space. She eased the mask back on his face and sat down. She resisted the urge to take his hand, instead, resting her hand on his wrist and stroking his arm. "What happened, babe?"

He closed his eyes and for a second, she thought he'd drifted off to sleep, but then he began speaking. "It was just a routine night. Instead of sitting at a DUI checkpoint, I was reassigned to patrol. Then we got a call: a driver had blown through a checkpoint and was flying down the expressway like a bat out of hell. I was on my way to assist another trooper who was helping a stranded motorist. I had just made the turn when the vehicle on the bulletin came flying down the road. He had to be going near 100, weaving in and out of traffic. Chicago Police were in pursuit and I joined in.

Then the driver slammed into the concrete median and spun out of control. He collided into a couple of cars. One of those cars went flying directly into Ben Williams."

"Is that the trooper that was killed?"

Jake nodded. "He couldn't get out of the way in time. He shoved the motorist he was assisting out of the way just in the nick of time."

Brianna shuddered. She could visualize the whole thing in her mind. "Did he have family?"

Jake shook his head. "Not a wife and kids. Just his parents and siblings."

"Did you know him well?"

"A little. I worked with him out of the academy for a few weeks. He was a good guy."

"Jake, how did you get hurt?"

"Once the cars were done crashing into each other, I pulled over and started helping the motorists. One of the cars was on fire, but there was a man inside. I was yanking on the door trying to get him out. Got a lung full of smoke. I got cut on some glass and burned my hands a little."

"A little?" She glanced at his heavily bandaged hands.

"Don't worry. I'll still be able to hold you close to me. But my MasterChef dreams will have to wait."

She laughed and a tear escaped from the corner of her eye. "I'll get Luis to make you some of his secret healing soup."

"The only thing I need to get me better is you by my side."

"You got that. Now and forever."

He pulled the mask off his face and gave her a curious look. "You mean that?"

She smiled. "Yes. The whole time I was waiting to find out if you were okay, I was praying for you, especially after I heard that a trooper had been killed. On the radio, we heard that a couple of people involved in the accident had been killed. They were minding their own business, driving to or from wherever, and their lives ended, completely unknown to them. And then God reminded me that ultimately, only He knows when our days will come to an end. He knows the day, the hour, and the manner in which we will die. The most important thing is we have a relationship with Him when it's our time to go. I was confident that if I never saw you again on this earth, I would see you again in eternity. That sense of peace made me realize that I wanted to be with you for the rest of my days—whether that's one day, one month, or fifty years. However, many days God gives us, it doesn't matter, as long as we can share them together."

Jake's grin grew wider. "What are you saying, Miss Norwood?"

Brianna's grin matched his. "I'm not saying anything, Mister Lewis. I'm asking if you will marry me."

Jake's grin evaporated. "No."

"No?"

"No. Not like this." He sat up out of his bed and swung his legs over the side. "Where is my shirt?"

"Wait a second. Where are you going?" Brianna asked. "You need to stay in bed."

"Not yet. Where is my shirt?" He climbed out of bed and stumbled to the entrance of the bay, where he flagged down a nurse. "Excuse me, what happened to my belongings?"

"They're in the cabinet," the nurse replied. "And you should be back in the bed."

"In a minute." Jake whirled around and moved toward the cabinet on the other side of the room. He found a plastic bag containing his belongings. He rummaged through them until he found his shirt.

"What are you looking for?" Brianna asked.

"Sit," he replied. "Sit, please." He waited until Brianna sat back down. He pulled out a small velvet pouch then turned back to face her. "I've dated women who were only interested in my badge. I've dated women who saw me as some sort of superhero or savior. But you're the first woman who saw me. From the moment we met, I knew you were different. And as I began praying for you, God slowly revealed that you were the one for me. But I had to wait until you were sure, until you were ready, until you were no longer afraid to love me without reservation." Slowly, he knelt down on one knee. "This is not how I had planned this, but it's as good a moment as any. This afternoon, I spoke with your father and asked for his blessing. Now, I'm asking you for yours." He emptied out the pouch revealing a diamond ring. "Brianna Norwood, will you marry me?"

CHAPTER THIRTY-FOUR

Lucille was wrong; it only took two weeks to plan a wedding. Neither Brianna nor Jake wanted an extravagant affair. They both agreed a simple ceremony with their closest family and friends was all they needed. What they couldn't agree on was how to merge their two households. Brianna argued that since she already owned her condo, it made sense for them to move into her home. Jake wanted Brianna to move into his building so he could retain his chef's kitchen.

In the end, since Jake had more than ten months on his lease, it would be easier for her to find someone to rent or buy the condo outright. They agreed to share his apartment until they could find a house they both loved. The only drawback was Brianna's commute would increase by twenty minutes, depending on traffic. On the plus side, she'd be able to park in the building's heated garage, which meant she wouldn't have to scrape off her car in the winter mornings.

Brianna found a renter in mid-July, which allowed her time to pack up her belongings and store them. She moved in with Liz and Luis, trading in free sitter help for rent. In August, she and Jake spent a week with her parents so she could help Lucille while she recovered from knee surgery. Brianna loved spending the time with her parents, learning more about what it meant to be a couple who were joined under the covenant of God. Ernest spent time counseling both Brianna and Jake, making sure they knew what they were signing up for before the ceremony. Lucille showed her daughter how to make some terrific family recipes that Jake immediately fell in love with. He couldn't wait to try them out in his kitchen and add his own personal flair to them.

After Trooper Williams' funeral, Jake pondered whether he should continue with his career. Ironically, it was Brianna who encouraged him to stay on and to train new recruits. He agreed to become a part-time instructor at the academy and a field training officer. He wanted the new troopers to know they weren't alone and they had a brother they could always depend on.

***

They opted to be married the day after her winter break began. The snow fell lightly on Jake and Brianna's wedding day. It was a hectic few days administering and grading finals as well as moving her things into Jake's—their—apartment, but Brianna didn't mind. Each night after work, she'd load up her car with things from storage and headed to the apartment. Jake cleared out part of his album and CD collection to make room for Brianna's desk and books. It was a little cramped, but Brianna was more than happy to share the space with her future husband.

Lucille, Julia, Alma and Liz joined Brianna in the bridal suite, assisting her as she slipped into her wedding gown, an off-the-shoulder ivory gown with a crisscrossed bodice and sweeping train. When she tried it on in August, the crepe material seemed too warm, but it was perfect for a winter wedding. The material hugged all of her curves in the right places and the sweetheart neckline accentuated her generous cleavage, causing Liz to let out a long, slow whistle.

"Girl, I don't know if Jake is gonna be able get through his vows when he sees you in this dress," she said.

"Oh, he'll get through them," Lucille said grinning. "Now whether or not they'll make it to the dinner is another story."

"Mom!" Brianna exclaimed.

"Honey, you're about to me a married woman. And as soon as you say your vows, you are free to do what married women do, whenever and wherever you want to do it."

"Oh my God," Brianna muttered, blushing. She rolled her eyes as the other women burst out laughing. "This is not the conversation I expected to have with my mother on my wedding day." She quickly changed the subject. "I have my something borrowed: Liz's diamond tennis bracelet."

"And you better not lose it," Liz said, giving her best friend a side hug."

"And here's your something new, *mija*," Julia said, handing Brianna a small box. "This is from Alma and me."

"We saw this and thought of you," Alma said. "You've been like a daughter to both of us. We wanted you to know how much we love you."

Brianna opened the box and let out a gasp. Inside lay a crystal and pearl choker with matching teardrop earrings. She blinked back tears. "You shouldn't have. I am so blessed to have you both in my life." As she hugged each woman, they whispered a prayer for her and Jake's happiness.

Lucille reached into her clutch. "Here's your something blue, my darling." She handed Brianna a small blue handkerchief, embellished by white lace. "Your grandmother gave this to me on my wedding day, as her mother had given it to her. On each corner, you can see the initials of the couple that were married. Yours and Jake's are on there now."

Brianna couldn't hold back the tears as she fingered the heirloom. "Oh Mom. This is beautiful. I love it, and I love you." She gave her mother a warm embrace.

"I know you'll treasure it. I hope that one day you'll be able to pass this on to your own daughter—or daughter-in-law, if God so sees fit."

"I will, Mom. Thank you." She hugged her mother again.

Liz fanned her face. "Look at you," she cried. "We're gonna have to do your makeup again." She walked over to the vanity in her velvet, wine-colored wrap dress. "As your matron of honor, I cannot have you going out there looking like you fell face first into a snowdrift."

Brianna laughed but followed her best friend to the lighted mirrored vanity and sat down. The other women, also visibly moved, began cleaning their faces and touching up their makeup, chatting giddily as the hour for the nuptials drew close. Liz deftly reapplied Brianna's makeup and touched up her lips to picture-perfect perfection. "Beautiful. If that dress doesn't knock Jake's socks off, your face will."

"I don't know what I'd do without you, Liz. Thanks," Brianna said. "And I'll make sure you get your bracelet back before we leave for Maui." She turned at the knock on the door to the suite. "That must be Dad. He's a bit early." She stood and opened the door. "What are you doing here?"

In the doorway stood Pete.

CHAPTER THIRTY-FIVE

Liz stomped over to the doorway. "Oh, I know you got some nerve showing your face around here, today of all days!"

"What are you doing here, Pete," Brianna asked again.

"You really shouldn't be here," Lucille added.

He waved. "Hey Mama 'Cille, Señora Julia, Señora Alma. Hi Liz. I'm not here to cause trouble."

"You are trouble," Liz said.

He chuckled. "Yeah, I do make an impression, although not the best one." He shifted his weight back and forth. "Look, I just want five minutes of your time. I promise to be on my best behavior. Just five minutes and I'll be out of your hair. Please, Brianna."

She sighed. "Okay, come on in. Five minutes."

"Are you crazy?" Liz hissed. "What if Jake finds out?"

"I'll tell him myself," Brianna replied. "And no one has to say anything to him about this." She closed the door then turned to face him. "You're on the clock."

"Can I speak to you in private?" he asked.

"Unh-unh! No way!" Liz said. "That's not happening."

"It's okay," Brianna said. "Go on. I'll be fine." She looked at her mother. "Please, Mom. Go tell Dad I'll be ready in ten minutes."

Lucille paused. "He's only got five."

"Five for him, five for me. If he goes one minute longer, I'll scream." She chuckled. "Please, ladies, go. You too, Liz."

"Fine," her friend replied. "But I won't be far." She turned her glare on Pete. "Luis is just down the hall," she warned through clenched teeth. She swung around and stomped out the door. Julia and Alma followed behind, muttering something angrily in Spanish.

Lucille started walking then stopped. "If you hurt my daughter—again—you don't have to worry about Luis, Ernest, or Jake. You understand me?"

Pete nodded solemnly. "Yes ma'am."

She nodded then kissed her daughter on the cheek. "Your father will be here to walk you down the aisle in ten minutes."

Brianna waited until her mother closed the door behind her before she spoke. "Why did you come here? In fact, how did you know I would be here?"

"A little birdie told me." At her raised eyebrow, Pete said, "One of our mutual acquaintances posted the details on Facebook."

"That still doesn't explain why you're here. On my wedding day."

"I came to say I'm sorry."

"You're sorry? Sorry for what?"

"I'm sorry for everything. I'm sorry for embarrassing you in front of your family. I'm sorry for going after your dad that day at the barbeque. I'm sorry for not respecting you and your beliefs. But most of all," he paused and took a step back, "I'm sorry that you're standing here, stunning as all get out, and you're giving yourself to another man instead of me. If I hadn't been such a fool—"

"We still wouldn't have made it, Pete. We want different things. We're on two different paths in our lives."

He nodded. "Maybe, maybe not. But you've made your choice, and I'll respect that. May I kiss the bride?" She nodded. He leaned in and gave her a peck on the cheek. "I always knew you'd make a beautiful bride. Barney Fife's a lucky man."

She laughed in spite of herself. "He's not lucky. We're blessed to have found each other. When you're ready, I hope you'll find the right one for you."

"Thanks." He shrugged. "I had the right one. I just wasn't smart enough to hold on to her. Take care of yourself, Bri. I hope you and Barn—Jake—are very happy together."

"Thank you, Pete. You take care."

He gave her hand a gentle squeeze then headed out the door. Brianna went to the vanity and checked herself in the mirror. She pulled a tissue from a box on the table. "Liz is gonna kill me if I ruin my makeup again." She dabbed at her eyes. "Father, I pray for Pete's heart, that he will really turn to you for guidance, for strength, and for peace. I pray you will direct his steps. I pray that when the time comes, he will find the woman you have designed for him. And I repent of the ways that I walked that were not of You. Please help me to be a good wife to Jake, the way he needs me to be, the way he deserves. Thank you for bringing him into my life for however long you see fit. Thank you, Father."

Another knock at the door, and Brianna's breath caught until she saw her father's face peeking around the corner. "Your mother said you might need a bit of a rescue."

Brianna exhaled and smiled. "I'm fine, Dad, but I'm glad to see you."

Ernest walked all the way into the room. "Oh, my goodness, Brianna. You are a beauty. I can't help but see my baby girl in you. But you're no longer a baby. You've grown into a lovely young woman. It makes my heart proud of who you've become. I'm so grateful that God sent you a good man in Jake. If I must give you away, I couldn't have picked a better man for you.

"Oh, Daddy," Brianna said. "Stop it." She dabbed at her eyes again. "I'm going to look like a raccoon."

"Not a chance. May I have the pleasure of walking you down the aisle?"

She went over and gave her father a squeeze. "I'd love nothing better."

CHAPTER THIRTY-SEVEN

Jake shook himself standing at the altar. He couldn't believe this was actually happening. He tugged at his tuxedo jacket nervously. Behind him, he could hear Desmond laughing. "Dude, relax. I've never seen you so nervous."

Jake turned around and rolled his eyes at his big brother. "You'll be nervous too, that is, if you ever find the right woman and decide to settle down."

"Not me, bro. I told you, I'm married to the Core." He smoothed down the jacket of his Marine dress blues. "Besides, Brianna is one of kind. And she doesn't have a sister, so that's out." The first strains of *Jesu, Joy of Man's Desiring* began playing. "This is it, bro. Showtime."

Jake nodded. He smiled as Liz walked down the aisle. In one hand she held a bouquet of purple roses. In the other arm, she carried little Bella. As the "flower girl," she didn't actually do much, except try to squirm away from her mother into her father's arms. Near the end of the aisle, Liz handed her daughter to Luis, who scooped her up and gave her a kiss. Liz reached the front of the altar and winked at Jake.

He turned back to face the minister. He knew what was coming next. He took a second to bow his head and offer up a prayer of thanks to the Heavenly Father for bringing them to this moment. He prayed he would always be worthy of Brianna's love and be able to protect her and love her the way she deserved.

He felt Desmond's hand on his shoulder. "Here comes your bride," he whispered.

Jake turned around and his mouth dropped. There were very few times in his life when he found himself speechless. This time, he was not only speechless, but breathless. "Steady bro," Desmond whispered, his hand bracing him from collapsing.

As long as I live, I will never forget this moment. Jake willed his brain to remember every single second as Brianna began her walk down the aisle of the church on her father's arm. If he never remembered what music was playing, who attended, or what anyone wore, the image of his fiancée was seared in his brain. The way her dress hugged every inch of her voluptuous body, he forced himself to not cry out in joy. As she made her way up the aisle, his grin grew wider and wider.

The minister began speaking, but Jake didn't hear the words. He couldn't take his eyes off of Brianna. It wasn't until Desmond poked him in the shoulder that he realized he was completely engrossed in her beauty. "What?"

"Answer the question," Desmond whispered in his ear.

Jake blinked. Brianna was staring at him with a furrowed brow. He glanced at his brother, who could barely conceal his smirk. He tipped his head towards the minister, who also held a bemused expression. "I'm sorry. What did you say, Reverend?"

"I asked if you, Jake Lewis, take this woman, Brianna Norwood, as your lawfully wedded wife, to have and to hold from this day forward; for better or for worse, for richer or poorer, in sickness and in health; to love, honor, and cherish, until death should separate you?"

Jake nodded eagerly. "Yes sir, I absolutely do."

***

The wedding guests were enjoying a sumptuous meal in a private dining room at the Signature Room at 95th in the John Hancock building. Most were marveling at the gorgeous city views as the city was lit up for the holidays.

Jake and Brianna ignored the views, as they were focused on each other. They were alone on the dance floor, swaying to a jazzy Branford Marsalis tune. Brianna had her head resting on her new husband's shoulder. She sighed.

"You okay, Mrs. Lewis?" Jake asked.

"I'm just fine, Mr. Lewis," she replied. "I was just thinking I hate to spoil this moment."

"You couldn't possibly spoil this moment."

She lifter her head and looked up at him. "I could if I told you Pete came to see me just before the wedding."

"I know."

"You know? How? Who told?"

"No one. I ran into him myself before the wedding."

"Is he in jail?"

Jake laughed. "If he is, it's not on my account. He apologized, wished us well. He said I was a lucky man. I told him I was— "

"Blessed," Brianna replied for him. "I thought you'd be angry."

"I'm not angry. He's a soul that needs Jesus. Besides, he's in the past. I'm only looking toward the future. And it starts right now." He leaned in for a kiss.

When they separated, Brianna gasped for breath. "Whoa, trooper. I may need to call 9-1-1."

"I'll rescue you anytime."

THE END

ACKNOWLEDGEMENTS

I am always amazed how stories seem to form from nothing. I do believe it's a prompting by God, especially when the I stall or try to do something other than write the story I've been given. I thank God for that push to get this story on paper.

My husband and son keep me rooted and grounded, but I know I have their love and support. I promise to give them my love and support always.

My niece Brianna was the inspiration for this heroine. I am so proud of the woman that you've become. The future is wide open, Brianna. Remember what I told you: be awesome!

Daphine and Cherlisa, my sounding boards, my fellow writers, my co-laborers on this journey: I feel like I've known you forever. I'm so glad God brought us together the way he did. I can't wait until we get together for our girlfriend writing retreat!

As always, I am grateful to you, the reader of this story. I hope you have enjoyed reading it as much as I enjoyed writing it. I thank you for your support, and encourage you to support other independent authors as they pursue their dreams.

If you've enjoyed this book, please spread the word! Leave a review on Amazon, Barnes & Noble, iTunes, or wherever you purchased this book. Feel free to say an encouraging word on your favorite social media platform. And reach out to me on Facebook, Twitter or Instagram.

OTHER BOOKS BY THE AUTHOR

Joy's Gift

Michele and Joy are as close as two friends can be without being related. The only issue they agree to disagree on is Joy's faith in Christ—and Michele's lack thereof.

A tragic accident leaves a hole in Michele's soul. In death, life begins for others as Joy gives the gift of her organs. But it is her final gift to Michele that may be the most valuable—hope for eternal life.

A Decent Proposal

Can money conquer all? Or will love get in the way?

Andrew Perry is days away from losing the shelter for teen runaways that he created. Without a new source of funding, the work he was dedicated his life to will be forfeited. He urgently prays for a way out. Wealthy socialite Vanessa Carson–Andy's ex– has a dilemma. In order to inherit her family's vast estate, and to protect her family's non-profit foundation, she has to be married by her thirti-eth birthday–ten days from now.

Vanessa approaches her former love with an unusual proposal: if he agrees to marry her for a year, she will fund his ministry for years to come. Desperate, Andy reluctantly agrees to the marriage– in name only. But there are those who will do anything to drive the couple apart–and those who want nothing more than to keep them together. With their faith, fortunes and futures inexplicably intertwined, Andy and Vanessa must decide what is most important to them–and whether it is worth the cost.

Journey to Jordan

Jordan Crawford has everything she's ever wanted—except peace.

A successful, ambitious, and focused attorney, she has done everything she had to do to escape the pain of her past. But one phone call sends her spiraling. As the memories of her family's legacy and her childhood unfold, Jordan's faith in people—and in God—is systematically shattered.

Yet, the further Jordan tries to run from God, the more He tries to draw her back. Unexpected reunions and circumstances force Jordan to take an emotional and spiritual journey through her tragic past—and into the promise of her future.

Made in the USA
Monee, IL
26 July 2025